KIRBY'S DILEMMA

A Novel by
Iris Iglarsh

Cover art:
Vera VonHoldenberg

For Charlotte and Edward Iglarsh,
who understood the greatest wisdom—kindness

Print ISBN: 978-1-66780-284-8

eBook ISBN: 978-1-66780-285-5

First Edition

CONTENTS

PART 1

Haunted

PART 1: HAUNTED

A WATERY VISION

I almost drowned when I was five years old. My family and I were on vacation in Ocean City, Maryland, with our cousins who lived nearby. I was walking along the shoreline of the Atlantic Ocean by myself, watching a few small waves trickle in, when a huge wave suddenly appeared and swept me into water above my head. I didn't know how to swim, and I was terrified.

As I drifted under the water, my brief life passed before my wide-open eyes. I waved my arms and kicked my legs wildly. That's when I saw a watery vision of a woman in a white gown. As she floated closer to me, even though we were underwater, I clearly heard her whisper to me, "Michael, don't be afraid, just believe in yourself."

A few seconds later, I heard a man's voice. He was yelling at me, but I couldn't understand him. The water was about three feet over my head, when the man swam toward me and pulled me back to the beach. There, he made sure that I was breathing, and then he walked away without saying a word.

Although I was petrified by the experience of almost drowning and seeing a ghost, I never told my parents. They had warned me not to wander too far away from them on the beach. If they ever knew what happened, I figured they'd probably watch me like hawks for the rest of my life.

As far as the lady in white who could speak underwater, I tried to convince myself that I had imagined her. Part of me, however, never let go of the possibility that she might have been real. And how did she know my name?

SIX YEARS LATER

On a chilly October evening, my parents, my brother, and I moved into our new house on Oakland Avenue in Long Field, Illinois. This happened a few days before I met Kirby. Our new home was a wood-framed, two-story house painted white that had been vacant for several months and was cold and drafty. After the movers left, my dad turned up the heat on the thermostat in the living room. As I watched, I saw a face reflected on the plastic cover of the thermostat. Dad didn't react to the reflection, so I assumed he didn't see it.

I wondered if I should mention the reflection, when it vanished. My family probably would have thought I was imagining things anyway. I also knew that Bryan would tease me mercilessly for saying something weird. At that time, my older brother always thought everything I said was weird.

"That's weird!" my dad said, still standing near the thermostat. "Do you hear that strange noise?"

Besides the wind howling outside and a few creaks in the hardwood floor, we all heard a distinct, repetitive squeaking noise. "Eee-awe, eee-awe, eee-awe…"

It sounded like a rusty spring doing an imitation of a braying donkey. When it stopped, everyone decided that the noise was coming from the heating vents, but I wasn't convinced.

"Oh boy," my dad said. "That's why I didn't want to buy an old house. My parents warned me there would always be something that needed fixing."

"But we fell in love with its *charm*. Right?" Mom straightened out the antique lace curtains in the living room. She had convinced Dad to buy an older house, even though his parents and her parents had warned them it would need a lot of work.

"Right," my dad said, rolling his eyes. "Let's all hit the sack and start unpacking tomorrow."

Looking forward to spending my first night in my new bedroom, I ran upstairs and got ready for bed in record time before my mom came to say goodnight.

As usual, she asked, "Did you brush your teeth?"

"Yep," I said, as she turned out the light.

"Wow, Michael! That's gotta be a record for the fastest time you ever brushed your teeth before going to bed. I'm amazed. You really must like it here. Don't you?"

"It's nice having my own bedroom," I said. "Goodnight."

"G'night," Mom said and kissed me on the forehead.

A RUDE AWAKENING

On Sunday, the second day in our new house, I woke up in unfamiliar surroundings and sat up like a shot. I wondered where I was and why my brother, Bryan, was missing.

When the sleepiness wore off, I happily realized that I was in the new house, alone in my own room. Best of all, there was no Bryan to whack me with a pillow, as he liked to do almost every morning.

At that moment, Bryan, who was much larger and more muscular than me, ran in and yelled,

"Hello, stranger!" as he started whacking me with a pillow he had brought in from his room.

"Stop it! Stop it! Get away from me! Get out of my room!"

"Okay, stranger. And I do mean 'strange.' See you later," he said and left my room.

After the early-morning abuse from Bryan, I crawled back into bed, put the covers over my head, and thought: *That's just my luck. I have my own room, but Bryan is still attacking me. I'm going to have to start locking my door.*

Under my quilt, which had illustrations of baseballs, basketballs, footballs, and soccer balls all over it, I heard the strange squeaking sound again, "Eee-awe, eee-awe." Only this time, I could hear it from the vent in my bedroom—not the living room. After the squeak, I heard a voice not much louder than a whisper say, "Get out of *my* room."

With that, I flew out of bed and down the stairs, almost slamming into the kitchen table.

"Hey, kiddo. What's going on? You look like you just saw a ghost," Dad said with a smile. He was already dressed and making coffee.

"No… um… I just need something to eat. Can I have some cereal?" I wasn't ready to tell anybody about what I had just heard.

While eating, I began to put the pieces together—the face in the thermostat, the weird squeaky noise, and the voice in my bedroom. I'd seen my first ghost when I was five, and now I could only come to one conclusion: *This house is haunted!*

FACE-TO-FACE ENCOUNTER

The next evening, as I sat on my bed doing sixth-grade social studies homework, out of the corner of my eye I saw a light-gray fog float in through the closed bedroom window. I was more curious than alarmed about this.

As the fog expanded, I watched it coil into what looked like an @ sign. That's when I stopped working on my laptop. A few seconds later, the fog changed into a pale-gray boy about my age, who had no color other than the various shades of gray that you would see in an old-time, black-and-white movie.

To see this gray ghost now—when I was hoping I'd never see another ghost again—totally freaked me out. I wanted to run, but I couldn't move. My leg muscles were frozen in fear, and I felt like my eyes were popping out of my head. As I watched the ghost float down to the floor, he looked at me straight in the eye and said, "Boo!"

That's when the rest of me responded. My bulging eyes led my body off the bed and over to the door, even before my laptop hit the floor.

I turned the doorknob and almost escaped, when the ghost yelled, "No! Stop! Stop! Don't run away! I was just kidding. Ghosts really don't say 'Boo.'"

If I had seen this ghost at my old house, I wouldn't have stopped running. But, because I already suspected that our new house was haunted, I stopped running and took a closer look at him. He was smiling and didn't look scary or dangerous.

I also noticed that my late-night visitor was dressed very formally and different from me. Instead of a T-shirt, jeans, and sneakers, he wore a suit with knee-length trousers, a button-down shirt, a necktie, and dark knee-high socks. His outfit reminded me of an old photo I had seen of my great-grandfather when he was a boy.

Hoping that I hadn't hurt the ghost's feelings by running away, I used my most polite voice to introduce myself. "My name is Michael Benton, and I'm not used to being around ghosts."

"Pleased to meet you. My name is Curtis Williams Scott, but Grandmamma and Mother called me 'Kirby.' The three of us used to live here, but now I'm the only one left. What are you doing in my room?"

His room? "Me and my family just moved here, and I was starting to wonder if this house was haunted."

"What made you think that?" Kirby asked.

As I picked up my laptop from the floor and sat on top of the bed, I told Kirby about seeing his reflection in the thermostat.

A DIFFICULT CHALLENGE

"Yes, that's right," Kirby said, after I told him how I figured out the house was haunted. We were now both sitting on my bed. "I'm especially proud of my face-in-the-thermostat trick."

"That was cool," I said. "How'd you do it?"

"I can't explain how I do it. I just think about it, and it happens."

"I wonder why I could see your face in the thermostat, but my dad couldn't."

"That's another thing I can't explain," Kirby said with a shrug.

"How old are you anyway?" I asked. "I'm eleven, and you look pretty close to my age."

"Well, I was born in 1934, but I died when I was eleven, so I never grew up. If I was alive today, I'd be about eighty years old."

"How did you die?"

"I'd rather not say. It's kind of embarrassing. What's that silver thing you dropped on the floor?" Kirby asked to change the subject.

"It's a laptop computer," I said and flipped it open. "Whew! I'm lucky it didn't break."

Scrunching his face close to the screen, Kirby asked, "What does it do?"

I didn't have the time or the desire to explain to my ghost friend how computers worked, so I gave a short answer. "Kids use laptops nowadays to do homework. It's electronic."

"Is the teacher inside of there, too?"

"No. My teacher, Ms. Frankel, still teaches in a classroom at my school. I need to give her the report

I'm working on by tomorrow morning," I said, looking at the clock on my nightstand.

"What's the report about?"

"Portuguese explorer, Vasco da Gama."

"Why are you doing a report on him?"

"Because Christopher Columbus, Juan Ponce de León, and Ferdinand Magellan were already taken."

"Ha, that's funny," Kirby said. "You seem pretty smart. Maybe you and your machine could help me figure something out."

"What's the problem?"

"I'm trying to find Mother. She died in this house, but her spirit hasn't come back. I miss her and want to know when she's going to return."

"When did she die?" I asked.

"I think it was last December, but I don't pay much attention to calendars. Do you think you could help me?"

With minimal experience at dealing with spirits, I answered: "Hmm. That's a tough one. Let me think about it. I'll try to help you, but not tonight. I need to finish my report. Is it okay if we talk more tomorrow?"

"Yes, of course. Finish your homework," Kirby said. "But please don't tell anyone else about me."

"You bet—if I told anyone, they'd think I was crazy. It's our secret."

And with that, Kirby transformed into a swirl of fog and disappeared before I could ask him any more questions.

After he left, I sat staring at the wall for about five minutes without moving. Was Kirby real or did I imagine him? Was the watery lady in white real or did I imagine her? Why had I already seen two ghosts in my life, when most people never see any? Did Vasco da Gama ever discover a ghost?

ASKED AND ANSWERED

I woke up the next morning thinking about Kirby. I hoped he was real, and that I hadn't imagined him. It surprised me that I wasn't scared anymore. I liked him because he was friendly.

Bryan—who was rarely friendly—and I were sitting at the kitchen table eating scrambled eggs and toast with our parents before heading off to school. Bryan left first to catch his bus to the junior high. But I still had a few minutes before I needed to leave for school. Our new house was much closer to Fieldview Middle School, so now I could walk there.

My parents, Anita and David Benton, were talking and laughing more than usual that morning. I guessed it was because they were happy with the new house. After all, they had worked hard to be able to afford it. Both of them were physical therapists, who had met in college. Now, they both worked for the same physical therapy group at different locations. I didn't have the heart to tell them that their new house was haunted. Besides, I had promised Kirby that I would keep him a secret.

My mom and dad were finishing breakfast before leaving for work, so I thought this was a good opportunity to get some information about Kirby's mother.

"Who lived in this house before we did?" I asked.

"Old Lady Sco…, I mean Mrs. Caroline Scott," my dad said. "She was over a hundred years old when she died. Her brother, George Williams, sold me the house. He's in his nineties and lives at the end of this block in the house with the white picket fence. Why do you ask?"

"Just wondering. See you later." I grabbed my backpack and walked toward the door.

"Bye," my mom said. "Be careful crossing the streets. Good luck with da Gama!"

AN EARLY DISCOVERY

Learning Caroline Scott's name was the first step in my promise to help Kirby find his mother's spirit. This discovery was a good start to my day, and to make my first walk to school more fun, I pretended I was exploring a new land. Would the natives be friendly? Were there any wild animals? What hidden treasures would I find?

The first "native" I saw was a tall, thin elderly man walking his dog. As I passed them on the sidewalk, I realized that they lived in the house with the white picket fence at the end of the block.

That must be Mr. Williams, Old Lady Scott's brother!

Pleased with the luck of my second discovery of the day, I sped off to school wondering what Kirby's family was like when he was eleven years old and alive.

CLASH MATES

"Michael, it's your turn," Ms. Frankel said, calling me up to do my Vasco da Gama presentation in front of my class at about ten o'clock that morning.

"Okay, I just need a minute to put on my costume," I said, as I reached into my backpack. The costume—an attempt to resemble a fifteenth-century explorer—consisted of my dad's floppy hat with a brim, a fake beard, and a vest. It wasn't the greatest costume, but I knew I would get extra credit points on my presentation for making the effort.

As I walked up to the podium, Ms. Frankel, a thin woman who looked younger than my mom, walked to the back of the room. She stood in front of a bulletin board that was covered with posters of European explorers. As I looked at the Vasco da Gama poster, he seemed to stare back at me with critical eyes. It was as if he was saying, "You look nothing like me with that ugly hat and fake beard." But he would have said it in Portuguese. Ms. Frankel looked far less critical as I faced the class, ready to start.

"Did you forget to shave this morning?" asked the pesky, pig-tailed Vickie Vargas, as the rest of the class laughed at her joke. If another kid had said that, I would have laughed. But, because everyone thought

Vickie had a crush on me, I was annoyed. To me, it seemed like she was trying to be the center of attention, even though I was the one in front of the class. And, because she and I got the top grades in school, we were always competing with each other.

My presentation went smoothly despite Vickie razzing me about the beard. I spoke slowly and used good eye contact to earn even more extra points.

"… and Vasco da Gama was the first European to reach India by sea," I said at the halfway point of my presentation. As I spoke, I could see that most of my classmates looked bored—the same way I probably looked when I listened to their reports. The only exception was Vickie. Sitting straight up near the front of the class, she was focused and staring right at me with eyes as dark as coffee beans. I avoided her stare and concluded my report.

Everyone in the class politely applauded when I finished. As I returned to my desk, Vickie said, "The hat was weird, but you did a good job."

"Thanks," I said, even though she was probably sure that her Juan Ponce de León presentation was better than my report on Vasco da Gama. Vickie had done a good job on her presentation earlier that morning, but the one thing she didn't do was wear a costume. Having that advantage over her gave me some comfort as I sat down and put my hat, beard, and vest into my backpack.

Vickie and I were competitive, especially in math. It amazed me how smart she was, but that only made me work harder. Besides, I was always careful not to hurt her feelings, because her father had died in a car accident last December, and I felt sorry for her.

We had been in fifth grade when our teacher, Ms. Edson, told us that Vickie's father had died. Everyone, including me, was shocked. Debbie Kahner, one of Vickie's best friends, started crying. I couldn't imagine what it would be like to lose a parent.

Now in sixth grade, as I walked home from school the day of my da Gama presentation, I realized that Vickie's dad and Kirby's mom had died in the same month. Having recently spoken to an actual ghost, I wondered if Vickie was able to talk to her dad's spirit.

If that was the case, and she had knowledge about the spirit world, maybe she could help me with Kirby's problem.

PART 2

Homework

A MEAN OLD MAN

The second time I spoke with Kirby, he appeared in my room as I was doing math homework at my desk.

"How'd your Vasco da Gama report go today?" he asked. I was impressed that he remembered my presentation or even cared.

"Not bad. I did my presentation in front of the class and turned in the report. My teacher, Ms. Frankel, hasn't graded it yet."

"Is that arithmetic?" Kirby asked, pointing to the paper I was working on.

"Yeah, but now we call it 'math,' which is short for mathematics."

"Gosh, you must really be smart to do that. I hope you can help me find Mother. I don't have much time left."

"What do you mean?" I asked and swiveled my desk chair around to look at him. He was standing next to my bed.

"When I was still alive, Grandmamma once told me that if a dead person doesn't come back as a ghost within a year of their death, they won't come back at all. Mother died in December of last year, and now it's already October."

"How did your grandmother know about the one-year deadline?"

"After my grandfather died, she wanted to talk to him, so she read a book about how to communicate with spirits."

"Was she ever able to talk with your grandfather's spirit?"

"I don't think so, but Mother and Uncle George inherited her interest in spiritualism."

"You know, I saw your uncle and his dog this morning as I was walking to school. If he knows something about spirits, maybe he could help us find your mom."

"Oh, not Uncle George! He's become a mean old man. He used to be nice, but now he's crabby and keeps to himself. As a ghost, I tried to visit him after his wife—my Aunt Maggie—died about twenty-five years ago. But I wasn't able to get through to him because he couldn't see or hear me. That made me sad, so I gave up."

"Do you think he would talk to me?" I asked.

"I'm not sure, but it would be very brave of you to try."

I liked the sound of that, so I replied, "Sure. This Saturday, I'll try to talk to him."

"That would be great. I'm going to leave now so you can finish your math. See you later."

"Kirby, wait a minute!"

"Yes?"

"There's another person I know who might be able to help us. Her name is Vickie, and she's in my class at school."

"Oh, really," Kirby said. "Is she your *girlfriend*?"

"Oh, jeez. Not you too! Everyone says she has a crush on me, but she annoys me."

"How could she help us?" Kirby asked.

"She's really smart, and her father died last December—the same month as your mother."

"I'm glad she's smart, but why would the same month make a difference?"

Desperate to come up with a more convincing argument, I said, "And her family celebrates the Day of the Dead every year."

"What's that?"

"It's a holiday celebrated in Mexico and other places where people pray for the dead and leave food and stuff for their spirits."

"Do you think she'll be able to talk to her dad's spirit on that holiday?"

"I'm not sure, but it's just another option we have to try to get help. I was thinking I'd tell her about you, but she'd have to keep it a secret. Would that be okay?"

"I don't know. Do you think she could keep a secret?"

"Yes. For me, I think she would."

"Wow! She must really like you," Kirby said. "Well … because I'm running out of time, I guess we should try it. The worst thing that could happen is that she'll think you're crazy."

"Maybe I already am."

"If you're crazy, then I don't exist. And I definitely exist, so you're not crazy. See you later. Let me know what Vickie says."

"Hey, Kirby. Before you go, I have one more question."

"Yes."

"Where do you go when you leave my room?"

"Um … I hope you won't think it's strange, but I go to the basement. There's a picture of Mother and me down there, and I like to look at it."

"Really? Where is it?" I asked, but there was no answer. Kirby had disappeared.

I wonder why he has so many secrets and why his uncle can't see him.

Thinking about Mr. Williams made my stomach ache. What would I say to him on Saturday? If he was as mean as Kirby said, maybe he'd have me arrested for trespassing or tell my parents that I was crazy.

And I didn't even want to think about what I would say to Vickie.

SATURDAY REPLAY

On Saturday afternoon, after hockey practice and lunch at Chipotle, I raked leaves in the front yard—my chore of the day. Somewhere nearby, I could hear the sound of a leaf blower and wondered why my family didn't have one. It would have made my job much more fun.

It was a nice day in late October, with the sun shining warmly on red and yellow leaves. As I raked, my mind wandered. I replayed that morning's hockey practice in my head. I did my best, but I wasn't as good as Bryan, even when he was my age, and that bothered me. To tell the truth, I was more interested in getting good grades in school than skating around in circles and whacking a puck past a goalie in a scary mask.

And why did I ever get involved in hockey in the first place? I guess the answer was that I didn't have a choice. My parents—both physical therapists and in great shape—made it very clear to my brother and me from an early age that physical activity was a "must do" in our family. Because my dad used to play hockey, when Bryan and I were old enough, they decided that we would join a junior hockey league.

That's why, on this Saturday morning after breakfast, Bryan and I went to hockey practice. I liked the game well enough, but Bryan was a more aggressive player. He liked the idea of body checking and leaving kids bruised and hurt on the ice. As for me, I never wanted to hurt anybody.

I wasn't too crazy about our coach, Mr. Weekly, either. Bryan thought he was a great coach, but that's because Mr. Weekly liked him. It seemed to me Mr. Weekly only liked the good players and gave them all of his attention. The average players—like me—were pretty much ignored.

The way I saw it—that was a problem. The coach was forever talking about teamwork and how we had to help each other out. For example, every November at our annual team party before the season started, Mr. Weekly would always give the same speech about team spirit.

I thought that if the coach had spent more time helping players like me, he would have had a better team. And it wasn't only me who felt that way. A lot of the kids thought Coach Weekly was a bully.

Still raking leaves, I started thinking about Kirby and his uncle, Mr. Williams. I tried to talk myself out of speaking to his uncle, but I didn't want to disappoint Kirby.

That meant I would have to walk over to Mr. Williams' house and ring the bell. The idea got my stomach churning because most people in my town didn't like to answer the doorbell unless they were expecting company. I learned this when I was selling candy bars door-to-door for my hockey team.

I also was nervous because Kirby said his uncle was mean, and I wondered if Mr. Williams would even open the door. Scarier yet, what if he did open the door? Who knows what would happen?

I was imagining the worst, when all of a sudden, I couldn't believe my eyes. There was Mr. Williams and his dog walking right past me as I was raking. Mr. Williams walked with a slight limp, and his head and shoulders were bent forward. The little bit of white hair left on his head looked like cotton puffs, and he wasn't smiling. His small, skinny dog was mostly beige-colored with black and brown spots. They both looked ancient.

"What's your dog's name?" I asked with a smile to start conversation.

There was no reply. Mr. Williams just walked by as if I wasn't there.

What a jerk! Kirby was right!

ANOTHER OLD MAN

The next day, my family and I had our regular Sunday brunch at my grandparents' house. I was always amazed at how my mom's parents, Jan and Martin Coin, were so different from my parents.

My parents were cool, calm, and well-mannered. Sometimes they would whisper to each other when they didn't want Bryan or me to hear what they were saying. They rarely raised their voices, kept our house clean and neat, and were so predictable that I often thought they were boring.

My grandparents, on the other hand, were less predictable. They spoke loudly most of the time and argued with each other frequently. Neither of them were in good shape because they rarely exercised, and their house was messier than ours. But they were undeniably more interesting than my parents, and would tell Bryan and me stories about their adventures when they were young.

As usual, we all ate brunch at my grandparents' kitchen table. When we were almost finished eating, I told my grandparents about my next writing assignment for my English class. They were always interested in my schoolwork, because both of them were retired high school teachers.

"Ms. Frankel wants us to write a story about our families," I told them. "So I'd like to get more information about both of you."

"This is going to be B-O-R-I-N-G!" Bryan said. He was not a big fan of history or almost anything else except hockey.

"Come on, Bryan," my mom said. "Everyone should know their family history."

"Okay," Grandma Jan said. "Tell me what you need to know."

"I'd like to start by learning more about Grandpa's dad," I said, as I pulled a small pad of paper and pen out of my jacket pocket. "Do you mind if I take some notes?"

"Not at all," Grandma Jan said. "Martin, you're the one who needs to tell him about your father."

"Well, your great-grandfather's name was William Bryan Coin," Grandpa Martin said.

"Is that who Bryan is named after?" I asked.

"Yep. And it's spelled the same way," added my mom.

"When my dad was twenty-five years old," Grandpa continued, "he married my mother, Martha Ann Miller, and thought it was the luckiest day of his life. Before that, he had been through a lot, including The Great Depression and being in the U.S. Navy during World War II."

"Where did he serve?" I asked.

"He served in Hawaii, where he maintained military aircraft. After the war, he found a job as a furniture salesman in Chicago and married his high school sweetheart, Martha. Life went on without any more major challenges for him. He liked it that way—quiet, happy, and with no conflict.

"Then they had kids, which changed everything," Grandpa continued. "I was born about a year after they were married, and your Great Aunt Ginny came along a year later. We weren't as quiet and cautious as our parents, and we were much more adventurous.

"If I wanted better job opportunities than my dad ever had, I knew I'd have to go to college. So I applied to a school not too far from home and started taking business classes in 1965. By the middle of my first year, I realized business school wasn't a good fit for me."

"He was too much of a free spirit to become a businessman," Grandma Jan said as she poured herself another cup of coffee.

"That's right. So I switched to biological science with plans to become a high school teacher. In one of my education classes, I met Jan Cooper," he said smiling at Grandma Jan. "She was studying to be an art teacher and was so smart and pretty that she knocked my socks off. You can take it from there, Jan."

"Never mind about the socks," Grandma Jan said with a smile. "Is this the kind of information you're looking for?"

"Yeah. This is great!" I said.

"B-O-R-I-N-G!" Bryan said.

My dad, who had been listening quietly, said, "Bryan, let's go into the living room to watch some football while they finish the story."

As Bryan and my dad left the kitchen, Grandma Jan continued.

"Martin and I were kindred spirits—both a bit on the wild side. Please don't use us as role models." She winked at my mom.

"A year later, we eloped against the wishes of both his and my parents because we were still in school and had very little money. When we returned from our honeymoon in South America, we took restaurant jobs to earn enough money to get us through college. After graduation, we both ended up with teaching jobs. A few years later, your mother was born. Her birth gave us great joy. And now, you and Bryan also give us joy."

"That's sweet," my mom said.

"Yeah. Thanks so much! This really helps," I said to my grandparents.

"Well, I hope your teacher likes it," Grandpa Martin said. "Now, I'm going to join David and Bryan in the living room."

As he walked away, I remembered there was something else I wanted to ask him. I followed him into the living room where the football game was on television, and the volume was loud.

"Grandpa." I said. But no response.

"Grandpa!" I said a little louder. But still no response.

"Martin!!" my dad said very loudly. "Michael is trying to ask you a question."

After my dad turned the volume down on the game, Grandpa Martin said, "Oh, I'm sorry, Michael. I guess I need to change the batteries in my hearing aids."

"That's okay. I was just wondering if you knew Mrs. Caroline Scott, who used to live in our house."

"That's the woman who lived to be over a hundred."

"Yep, that's her. Do you know if she had any kids?"

"Not sure, but her brother, George Williams, would know. He lives down the street from you. You should ask him."

I was about to explain how Mr. Williams had ignored me when he walked past my house less than 24 hours earlier. That's when I realized that maybe Mr. Williams—who was even older than my grandpa—hadn't heard me because he was hard of hearing, too.

"That's a good idea," I said. "I'll ask him. Thanks."

ONE-WORD ANSWERS

On Monday afternoon, when I returned from school, my mom met me at the door to our house. She was still in her work clothes, which made her look like a doctor wearing scrubs. I could tell she was tired because she was loosening the elastic band around her ponytail. She always let her hair down when she was tired.

"Hi, Michael. How was your day?"

"Fine," I said, using the one-word-answer technique I learned from Bryan. I didn't feel like talking much because I was thinking about how to handle the Kirby situation with his uncle.

Trying to encourage conversation, my mom asked, "Did anything interesting happen at school?"

"Nope," I answered with another classic Bryan response.

"So anyway," she continued, sounding a little frustrated, "I called the heating and air conditioning guy today, and he's coming to check the furnace tomorrow because of that weird noise we heard when we moved in. With the cold weather coming, I want to make sure it's working right."

"Oh … um … th-th-that's good," I said, even though I was pretty sure it was Kirby who made that noise in the basement. "Um … I'm going to … uh … play outside a little before dinner. Okay?"

"That's fine. See you later."

PLOTTING A STRATEGY

After my mom told me that the furnace guy was coming, I walked outside, feeling that my two worlds—the one with Kirby and the one with my family—were about to collide. I also worried that the furnace guy might scare Kirby away. Our deadline for Kirby to find his mom was getting close, and I began to feel that Mr. Williams and possibly Vickie were the only two people who could help. I couldn't talk to my family about Kirby, because he asked me not to. But it was getting harder and harder to keep him a secret from my parents.

I tried to figure out how I could meet with Mr. Williams. The odds of running into him on the street again seemed low. There was no choice. I had to walk to his house and ring his doorbell. The only question was: What would I say?

Obviously, "Hello, Mr. Williams, do you know how the spirit of Kirby can find the spirit of his mother?" wasn't going to work.

And what would I say to Vickie to get her on board? How could I reveal Kirby's secret to her? Would she then blab it to the whole world?

As I considered my bizarre situation, an idea came to me—an idea I would have to check out with Kirby.

PAN DE MUERTO

"Now that we've finished the European explorer unit," Ms. Frankel said, standing in front of the class the next day, "we're going to spend a few days learning about the Mexican holiday, Day of the Dead. This is the perfect time to learn about this observance, because the first day of this three-day holiday falls on Halloween. Does anyone want to share what they already know about the Day of the Dead?"

Vickie Vargas, of course, was the first to raise her hand. She was enthusiastic about this study unit because her mother was born in Mexico, and her father's parents also came from Mexico. That's why she considered herself to be the expert on everything Mexican.

"During the Day of the Dead—or *Día de los Muertos* in Spanish—people pray for their relatives who have died," Vickie said. "And people build private altars filled with the favorite food and drinks of their dead relatives."

"That's right," Ms. Frankel said. She was holding a stack of papers and walking over to the olive-green wall on the left side of the classroom. "And besides food and drinks, families often bring bright orange marigolds and *calaveras,* which are tiny decorated skulls made out of sugar or clay."

"We sell those at my family's grocery store," Vickie said. "And we also make *pan de muerto.*"

"I'm glad you mentioned that," Ms. Frankel said, "because I'm handing out the recipe right now. *Pan de muerto* means 'bread of the dead,' and if you bake it with a parent and bring your loaf to school on Halloween, you'll get five extra credit points."

I liked hearing that because I was always a sucker for extra credit.

As my class walked to the cafeteria for lunch, I asked Vickie if she was going to make *pan de muerto* for the holiday.

"Of course," she said. "My mother's going to teach me how to make the bread tomorrow after school, and we're going to get some sugar skulls from our Mexican grocery store."

"I'm going to ask my mom to help me make *pan de muerto*, too," I said. "We've never done that before."

"Hey, Michael," Vickie said with a sparkle in her eye. "How about coming over to my house tomorrow to help me and my mother make the bread of the dead? She makes it every year, and she even knows how to make the bread look like a skull and cross-bones. It's kind of creepy, but cool."

The idea of going to Vickie's house scared me. It wasn't because of the bony bread, but because everybody already teased me about Vickie being my girlfriend. If anyone knew that I went to her house to bake bread, they'd tease me even more.

On the other hand, it sounded like fun—making bread that looked like bones. And it would give me a chance to check out any Day of the Dead secrets about how to talk to spirits. In the end, I took the brave choice and accepted her invitation.

REGULAR VISITS

Kirby started visiting me in my room almost every night. We would sit on my bed and talk quietly. He somehow knew the best times to show up when there was less chance of someone in my family coming near. And he was very considerate about not interrupting me when I had a major homework assignment.

It was now more than a week from when we first met, and I decided that he was comfortable enough with me that I could ask him some personal questions.

"Kirby, right now I can see you as a ghost, but I've also seen you as a swirl of fog, and sometimes you're invisible. How do you switch like that?"

"All I do is think about what form I want to take, and it happens," Kirby said. "It wasn't easy at first when I was a new spirit, but with practice I got better at it."

"And how do I know that you're not spying on me when you're invisible?"

"You're going to have to trust me on that one, the same way I trust that you won't tell your family about me. I'll only go invisible around you when there's a chance other people might see me. It's like when I lived with my mother for almost seventy years as a ghost. She never told another living soul about me."

"I forgot that you've been a ghost for such a long time."

"It's been so long now," Kirby said, "that I stopped paying attention to clocks and calendars. Only now, I'm paying closer attention because of the deadline for my mother to come back as a spirit."

"Was your mother scared when she first saw you as a ghost?"

"Well, I was a much less experienced ghost then, so I hung around the graveyard for the first three years. Every Sunday, Mother would come to the cemetery to visit the graves of Grandfather, Grandmamma, and me. I always stayed invisible so I wouldn't scare her.

"On Sunday, October 17, 1948, in my invisible form, I decided to follow my mother as she walked home from the cemetery. I wanted to be with her because it was her birthday.

"When she turned onto our street, Oakland Avenue, she heard a rustle of leaves that startled her. Back in those days, there was more farmland around here, and there weren't as many houses on the block or people on the street.

"As she walked up the deserted street, she passed Uncle George and Aunt Maggie's house. They were newlyweds at the time and not home. Their gate rattled in the wind as Mother walked by, which also startled her. Somehow, I think she sensed she was being followed, so she picked up her pace and rushed home.

"In the house, she made a cup of tea to calm down. I watched as she sat on the living room couch to read the Sunday newspaper. As she read, she became drowsy and almost drifted off to sleep. That's when I decided it was time to materialize. As I appeared, I quietly said, 'Hello, Mother. Don't be afraid. It's me, Kirby. Happy Birthday!' It was good she was sitting down because, when she saw me, she fainted."

"Oh, no!" I said. "Was she okay?"

"Yes," Kirby continued. "When she woke up, I was sitting at the other end of the couch, relieved that she had only been out for a few minutes. I told her that I wasn't sure how to show myself without scaring her. I also explained that I had watched her at the graveyard every Sunday for a long time and decided to come back home on her birthday.

"Later that day, my mother told me that I was the best birthday present ever, but she couldn't believe I was back. I assured her that she could believe it and I wanted to be with her forever. She questioned if I could do that, and I didn't really know. But I stayed with her until she died last year, and that's the story," Kirby concluded.

"Wow, that's an awesome story!" I said.

"Yes, Michael. It's a story that only you, me, and Mother know about."

"Don't worry, your family secret is safe with me. And speaking of family, I figured out a way to get a chance to talk to your uncle."

"Really? How?" Kirby asked.

"Well, Halloween is coming up in two days, and I'm going to trick-or-treat at his house. Do you know what trick-or-treating is?"

"Of course. When I was alive, I used to dress up as a ghost and always got good treats. Now, I don't need a costume."

"Very funny," I said. "Do you think my plan will work?"

"Not really," Kirby said honestly. "Uncle George probably won't even open the door and talk to you, let alone give you any candy. But we're running out of time, so anything is worth a try."

"I agree. I think it's worth a try."

"Wow, Michael. You're really brave. What's your costume?"

"I still have the Vasco da Gama outfit I wore when I did my social studies report in front of the class."

"That's different," Kirby said. "I'm sure no one else will be wearing *that* costume. I'd go to his house with you, but I know my uncle won't be able to see me."

"At least you'd hear what he had to say."

"No, that's all right. I don't want to be disappointed again. Just let me know how it goes."

PART 3

Holiday

PART 3: HOLIDAY

DAY OF THE BREAD

On the day before Halloween, Vickie and I walked to her house after school. It was a surprisingly warm fall day, so we took our time instead of rushing to get out of the cold. Vickie's street was lined with houses on both sides, just like mine.

My mom liked the idea of me baking bread with Vickie and her family. She asked me to give her a call when I was ready to be picked up so I wouldn't have to walk home alone in the dark. Bryan was also at a friend's house that evening. I was worried that if he ever found out I was at Vickie's house, he'd tell the whole world and tease me forever.

Besides baking the bread and getting extra credit for it, another major reason I wanted to go to Vickie's house was to see if she knew any Day of the Dead secrets. I wondered if she had a way to speak with her father's spirit. But I'd have to be careful about the way I asked her my questions. It wasn't even a year since her father's death.

As we walked, I decided that this was the best chance I'd have to tell her about Kirby.

"Vickie, I have to tell you a secret that you can never tell anyone else."

This got her attention, and I blurted it out before I lost my nerve. "I know you're going to think I'm crazy, but my house is haunted, and I'm friends with a ghost."

That made Vickie's eyes pop.

"Are you joking or trying to scare me?" she asked.

"No. You have to believe me. This is serious, and I need your help. That's why I'm telling you. But you have to keep it a secret for Kirby's sake."

"Is that the ghost's name?"

"Yes. He and his mother used to live in my house."

"Whoa! I've heard about people living in haunted houses, but I never believed it. Are you sure you're not imagining things?" Vickie asked, as we reached the front door to her house.

"I'll tell you more later, but we can't talk about it with your family listening."

"Okay, but that's all I'm going to be thinking about."

As we walked into her house, we were greeted by Mrs. Vargas and Vickie's younger sister, Mia.

Her mom looked like an older, larger version of Vickie, with dark, thicker hair that she wore in a bun, which included some strands of gray.

Mia, who was eight years old, was extremely friendly and bouncy, like a bunny that never stopped hopping. I'd never met Mia before, but she was gushing all over me like I was special.

"Are you *Michael*?" Mia asked. "Vickie talks about you all the time."

Vickie and I were both embarrassed by this, so I started talking to their mom. "Hi, Mrs. Vargas. Thanks for letting me come over to learn how to make pan de muerto."

"Can I help? Mommy! Can I help?" Mia shrieked as she jumped up and down, pulling on her mother's apron.

Vickie said nothing, which was unusual. She just kept looking at me suspiciously.

"Let's all go into the kitchen," Mrs. Vargas said. "I want to show you what I've already done."

It turns out that to make the dead bread you have to let the dough rise for an hour or two before you can bake it. Mrs. Vargas had taken care of this ahead of time, so we wouldn't have to wait so long.

That meant she had already mixed all the ingredients in with the flour and the yeast, and the dough had risen. All we had to do was punch the dough down, shape it, bake it for about forty minutes, and then brush it with a sugary, orange juice glaze.

Because I was the guest, Mrs. Vargas gave me the honor of punching the dough.

"Don't hurt your hand or break the bowl," Mia giggled.

As I punched the sticky, squishy dough down into the bowl, Mia screamed with joy as if it was the funniest thing she had ever seen. Vickie still said nothing.

Then, we all helped shape the bread into two loaves that both looked like the skull and crossbones symbol on pirate ships. When we made the teeth for the skull out of little pieces of dough, Mia giggled again. When we shaped the dough to look like crossbones, Mia said they looked like big dog bones. One of the loaves was for Vickie's family, and the other was for me to take home.

POSING A DELICATE QUESTION

After we put the bread in the oven, we had about forty minutes to wait. Vickie and I, without Mia, went downstairs to play ping-pong in their finished basement. The light wood paneling and beige carpeting made their basement look much less creepy than mine. The most prominent pieces of furniture were the green ping-pong table and an orange sofa that had seen better days. Above the sofa, a large family photo of Vickie and Mia with their parents was hanging on the wall. I paused to look at their father.

As soon as we got downstairs, Vickie exploded with questions.

"Were you lying to me about the ghost thing?"

"No. I swear it's true."

After I told Vickie the whole story about Kirby and his struggle to find his mom's spirit, she said, "I want to meet him."

"Okay, I'll try to introduce you to him, but you've got to keep him a secret. He's shy about meeting people because he's afraid they'll blab about him all over town. I'm hoping that if I let him know you're willing to help, he'll want to meet you."

"I'm not sure how I'll be able to help, though," Vickie said. "What do you plan to do?"

"We need to find a way for Kirby to contact his mom's spirit. He misses her terribly, and I promised

I would help him. I'm going to check with Kirby's uncle, Mr. Williams, who lives on my street. Kirby thinks his uncle may know something about talking to spirits."

"What can I do to help?" Vickie asked, scratching her head with the ping-pong paddle.

Here's where I had a chance to ask for what I wanted, but I knew I had to handle it carefully. "Well, your mom seems to know a lot about the Day of the Dead. Do you think she knows how to speak with the spirits of the dead when they come for their favorite food and beverages at the altar?"

Vickie was quiet for a few seconds before she said, "I wonder if I would be able to talk to my dad."

"Do you think you could ask your mom?"

"I'll ask her tonight after Mia goes to sleep. But can I ask you a favor in exchange?"

"Sure."

"Would you be able to read my family story that I wrote for English class? I think it's good, but I'd like to know what you think."

"No problem. Just email it to me and I'll look at it," I said. "Do you want to play some ping-pong now?"

"Fine, but I'm warning you, I'm pretty good."

We played competitively until we heard Mrs. Vargas at the top of the basement stairs. "Vickie! Michael! The bread is ready!"

With that, we put down the paddles and ran up the stairs to look at the golden-brown loaves.

"Mmm! That smells good!" Mia said. She was already in the kitchen helping her mother spread the glaze on the loaves.

The sweet, warm smell of the bony bread, fresh out of the oven, made me hungry and reminded me that it was almost dinner time. While the bread was cooling, I called my mom to arrange for a time to pick me up.

When my mom showed up in her car, Mrs. Vargas gave me my loaf wrapped in plastic.

"Thanks, Mrs. Vargas. It was fun helping with the bread. And Vickie and I will get extra credit for taking the bread to school tomorrow. Bye, Vickie! Bye, Mia!"

All three of them said their goodbyes at the same time, but Mia was the loudest.

WALKING IN THE NIGHT

That night, I read Vickie's story.

A Ringing in My Ears—My Family Story
by Victoria Luna Vargas

Thirty years ago, my mother, Melita Luna, came to the United States from Mexico. She was eleven years old when she came with her parents and her younger sister, Maria. What my mother remembers most is walking long distances through deserts, and how cold it was when they walked at night.

After walking and getting rides in trucks and buses, they arrived in Illinois, where my grandfather had a cousin. Fourteen years later, my mother married my father, Daniel Vargas, who was born in the United States from Mexican parents.

I was born two years later, and my younger sister, Mia, was born three years after that. When Mia and I were old enough to go to school, my mother started to feel comfortable in the United States. She could speak English fluently and made friends with other mothers in the neighborhood. But she rarely spoke about her long, cold, scary walk in the night.

When I was in fifth grade, Dad dropped me off at school on a snowy day in December. I usually walked to school, but when the weather was bad, Dad would take me on his way to work. Dad and Uncle Leo owned a small Mexican grocery store that was 15 miles from our house. He drove the green "Vargas Grocers" van when he dropped me off at school. As I opened the van door to get out, my father told me he loved me.

An hour later, Mr. Miller, the assistant principal, knocked on the classroom door during my English class. He came in and asked my teacher, Ms. Edson, if she could speak with him in the hallway.

Ms. Edson walked out to talk with him. A few minutes later, she came back to the classroom and asked me to join her and Mr. Miller in the hallway. I was scared and had no idea what was going on.

In the hallway, Mr. Miller got straight to the point: "Vickie, your aunt just told me that your father was in a traffic accident on his way to work this morning. I know the roads were very slippery, but I don't know exactly what happened. He was taken to the hospital, and your mother is with him."

"Is he okay?" I asked, trying not to cry.

"I don't know his condition right now. But your aunt will take you and your sister to the hospital."

As Ms. Edson put her hand on my shoulder to comfort me, I wondered how it happened and how badly he was hurt. I worried that it was my fault because it happened after he dropped me off at school.

My aunt was parked in front of the school, and Mia was already in the back seat of the car. As I joined her in the back seat, I could tell Mia was scared. We hardly spoke on the way to the hospital. All my aunt said was that when we got there, we'd find out what happened and how my dad was doing.

At the hospital, my first eye contact with my mother made my heart freeze.

"Is he okay?" Mia and I asked. "Is he okay?"

"No, my angels," my mother replied. "He didn't make it."

We were all too shocked to cry.

"I'm going to say goodbye to Daddy in the hospital room," my mother said. "Do you want to come in with me?"

We followed her in silence and saw my dad lying on the bed with machines all around him. The top of his head was wrapped in bandages.

"Why does he have that thing on his head?" Mia asked.

"Because Daddy hurt his head before they brought him to the hospital," my mother said.

That's when my ears started ringing. It wasn't loud, but it sounded like a tiny motor running inside my head. I was hoping that somehow he would miraculously open his eyes and sit up, so we could all walk out of the hospital together.

But he didn't move, and the ringing in my head didn't go away. That's when I knew deep down that he would never walk, talk, or give me a hug again.

"Is it okay if I touch him?" I asked my mother.

"Yes, sweetie, that's fine."

I took my father's right hand and held it tightly while standing near the bed. Mia ran to the other side of the bed and held his left hand. My aunt was at the foot of the bed, and my mother was standing near me closer to my father's head. We stood there for a long time crying and quietly saying goodbye. My mother kissed him on the part of his forehead that wasn't covered with bandages.

The ringing in my ears finally stopped when we left the hospital. I came away thinking that the ringing was my father's spirit telling me that everything was going to be all right, but I would need to help my mother and take care of my sister.

After reading Vickie's story, it took me a long time to fall asleep. I was amazed at how much I didn't know about her and impressed by how well she told her family story.

I wondered what I would do if I lost one of my parents. Would I hear the ringing, too?

I finally fell asleep thinking about how different my family history was from hers. I guess everyone has their own story to tell.

PART 4

H ALLOWEEN

PART 4: HALLOWEEN

HALLOWEEN SPIRIT

I never understood why some kids like Todd Schultz would wear the same Halloween costume every year until it didn't fit anymore. And sure enough, this Halloween, Todd wore the same one for the third year in a row. His costume, which his mother made, was a big hit the first year he wore it to school. Maybe that's why he liked it so much. But now, it was the third year I'd seen his fake third arm coming out of his chest, and I didn't find it funny anymore. Plus, the costume was getting too tight on him.

I think he was supposed to be a Martian, because he wore a clear, round plastic helmet with two antennas sticking out of the top. And his silver space suit had sleeves for three arms—his real arms and the fake one. He looked like a cartoon version of a plump Martian. If I ever get the chance to meet a real Martian, I doubt it would look anything like Todd with three arms.

Other boys had store-bought costumes of Batman, Spider-Man, Superman, and other super-heroes. The boys with homemade costumes usually went with the sports theme as a baseball, football, hockey, or soccer player. No one but me showed up as a European explorer. I got a lot of razzing about recycling my Vasco da Gama costume, but it didn't bother me because I thought that collecting candy was more important than costumes.

For the girls, outside of the usual black cat and witch costumes, some of the ideas were pretty clever. Debbie Kahner dressed up as a cell phone. Paula Carrell was a yellow M&M's Peanut Candy. Vickie Vargas was a Gryffindor Girl, wearing the black robe, white button-down shirt, and red and gold tie that Hermione Granger and other characters wore in the Harry Potter movies.

As we walked back to our classroom after lunch, the Gryffindor Girl caught up with me and reported on what her mother had told her about talking to spirits.

"My mother said that my family won't be able to see or speak directly to my dad's spirit, but we will feel his presence with us."

"Hmm, that's good to know," I said, "but it probably won't help Kirby."

"I wonder why you can see and talk to Kirby's spirit, but I can't see my dad."

"I think it's because very few people come back as ghosts," I said. "I mean, if everyone did, we'd see crowds of ghosts all over the place."

"So why is Kirby special?" Vickie asked.

"Not sure."

"Didn't you say that Kirby's uncle is supposed to know about spirits?"

"That's what Kirby told me," I said. "I'm going to trick-or-treat at his uncle's house tonight to see if I can get some information from him."

"That's brilliant!" the Gryffindor Girl said. "I'd go with you, but I'm trick-or-treating with Debbie and Paula tonight. Did you get a chance to read my family story?"

"I read it last night, and it's really good. I'm sure you'll get an A-plus on it."

"Thanks. If you want, I could read your story, too."

"No. That's okay. It's not as interesting as yours."

"Well, if you change your mind, let me know," Vickie said, as the bell rang for our next class. "And let me know what happens with Kirby's uncle. Happy Halloween!"

CANDY STRATEGY

After school, I ran home superfast so I could get ready for trick-or-treating as soon as possible. My family had spent a couple weeks preparing for Halloween. We decorated our front yard with fake spider webs, tombstones, and images of ghosts, which looked nothing like Kirby. We also bought the "good" kind of candies—meaning anything with chocolate in it.

This year, the costumes were easy to put together. I already had everything I needed to be Vasco da Gama again, but we added a few extra touches. My costume consisted of the large floppy hat, the fake mustache and beard, a red vest over a black sweatshirt, a wide leather belt that was way too big for me, black sweatpants, and black snow boots. Not surprisingly, Bryan was dressed as a hockey player with a scary, white goalie mask.

I was going to trick-or-treat with the O'Connor twins, Billy and Brad, who lived a block away. Bryan was going with his hockey buddies. I planned to stop at Mr. Williams' house on my way home after splitting off from Billy and Brad. Because I would be going to the mean guy's house alone, I expected this to be the scariest Halloween of my life.

After adjusting my costume and grabbing the biggest shopping bag I could find, I started walking over to the twins' house. The streets in my neighborhood were already crowded with kids of all ages going door to door. The younger ones were with their parents, and I was proud I had reached an age where I could trick-or-treat without adult supervision.

I met the twins—dressed as Iron Man and Spider-Man—in front of their house. As soon as I walked up to them, Brad asked me, "How come you're not trick-or-treating with *Vickie*?"

"Isn't she your *girlfriend*?" Billy joined in. And they both started laughing.

"Come on guys, she's not my girlfriend, and I always trick-or-treat with you. Let's get going. I want to collect as much candy as possible in the next two hours."

"Okay," Billy said. "Before we head out, let's decide what we want to do. Do you think it would be faster if we stick to one side of the street and then do the other side? Or should we zigzag back-and-forth?"

"I think we should stick to one side and then the other," Brad said. "That way, we won't have to cross the street so many times and have to wait for cars driving by. What do you think, Michael?"

"I think we should do one side at a time and run really fast between the houses," I said. "If it looks like nobody's at home, we just run past that house so we can get to as many good ones as we can." The houses with the best candy were the "good ones."

We were just about to get started, when we saw a three-armed, chubby Martian running up Brad and Billy's driveway.

"Hey, guys! Wait up!" yelled Todd Schultz, who lived across the street from Billy and Brad. "Can I join you?"

"Sure," Billy said.

"But you have to keep up with us," Brad said.

"We want to get to as many houses as we can," I said.

"Fine," Todd said. "The more candy, the better."

Two hours later, with a heavy bag of treats, I parted company with the twins. We had lost track of Todd after he had slowed down an hour earlier and told us to go on without him. Now, I was on my mission to meet Mr. Williams.

TRICK OR DEFEAT

It was getting dark as I approached Mr. Williams' house. No pumpkins, fake spider webs, or any other Halloween decorations were on his front lawn. All I saw were tall, faded plants and grasses blowing eerily in the wind.

As I opened Mr. Williams' gate, its squeak startled me. I began to fear he might kidnap me and keep me in his basement. That's when I realized Kirby and Vickie were the only two souls who knew I was going to Mr. Williams' house. In hindsight, I thought I probably should have told my parents.

I saw a glimmer of light inside the house, so I knew Mr. Williams was home. Forcing myself to keep moving, I walked past the bushes in his front yard, climbed the stoop to his front door, and put my pointer finger on the doorbell. But I was too nervous to press the buzzer.

I considered leaving right then and there. And I'm sure I would have, if it wasn't for Kirby. I didn't want him to think I was chicken. Besides, what would I tell Vickie the next day after she thought my idea was so brilliant? So I took a deep breath and rang the buzzer twice, causing Mr. Williams' dog to bark.

After what seemed to be an excruciatingly long time, Mr. Williams opened the large wooden door and looked outside through the glass pane of his storm door. He was wearing wire-rimmed glasses, a gray sweater, and khaki pants. I could see that he was tall and slim, but his shoulders were slumped over as he looked through the glass.

"Trick or treat!" I yelled with so much force that my Vasco da Gama hat slipped down over my eyes.

"What?" Mr. Williams asked, as he opened the storm door a crack to hear me.

I pushed my hat back up and said, "Trick or treat! You know—Halloween and all that stuff."

"Oh, I'm sorry," Mr. Williams said. "I was cooking dinner, and you took me by surprise. I don't usually get trick-or-treaters."

At that moment, his dog showed up, looked through the glass pane and gave a high-pitched bark.

Feeling more at ease, I asked, "What's your dog's name?"

"His name's Duke, and I'm George Williams," he said, as he walked outside to talk to me and shake my hand. Duke followed and gave me his paw.

"Nice to meet you. I'm Michael Benton, and my dad told me that we bought our house from you."

"Oh, yes. That's right. How do you like the house? It used to belong to my sister, Caroline."

"It's fine, but I was wondering where your sister moved to." I, of course, knew she had died, but I thought it was a good way to start talking about Kirby's mom.

"She didn't move. Unfortunately, she died last year."

"Do you think her spirit will ever come back to my house?"

"It's funny you should ask. My mother, sister, and I used to be interested in spiritualism—communicating with the dead. In fact, at one point I thought I had seen the ghost of someone I knew. I wanted to reach out to him, so I began to do more research on spiritualism."

Mr. Williams looked at me as if he was about to tell me something very important, but then thought better of it. So I tried to pry more out of him.

"Were you successful?"

"No," Mr. Williams replied. "I gave up because I got scared."

"Scared of what?"

"Scared that I would … well … never mind. You don't have to worry about my sister coming back to haunt your house. Although, sometimes I think that very strong spirits hang around because they aren't ready to leave this world. But Caroline had a long, full life, and I think she was ready to go."

Aha! This was an answer to Vickie's question about why Kirby was so special that he came back as a ghost. I wondered why Kirby's spirit was so strong, and why he didn't want to let go.

"Did your sister have any kids?" I also knew the answer to this question, but I wanted to learn more about Kirby.

"Um … yes," he said with a sad pause. "She had one boy, my nephew Kirby, who died when he was eleven."

"That's how old I am right now. Was he sick?"

"No. It was a tragic, terrible accident. It happened on a Sunday morning before the family was leaving for church. He was jumping on a pogo stick and fell down the basement stairs."

Stunned by the news, I said, "Oh man, that's really sad."

"I know. It still hurts to think about it after so many years."

"Wow, I'm so sorry."

"He was my only nephew, and I was like a father to him because his real dad wasn't around."

"What happened to his father? Did he die, too?"

"He died about twenty years ago, but he and Caroline had split up way before then, when Kirby was a baby," Mr. Williams said with a faraway look in his eyes.

At that point, I thought it would be best to stop asking questions because Mr. Williams looked so sad. "Well, I have to head home for dinner now, but it was nice talking to you."

"What about your candy? You're not going to leave without a treat, are you?" Mr. Williams opened the storm door briefly to grab something inside. "My daughter, Roseann, brought me this candy in case I had any trick-or-treaters. I told her I wouldn't get any, but she left the treats anyway. Do you like Scottish Fish?"

"Sure," I said, as I took a small bag of candy, which was really called "Swedish Fish," but I didn't think it was necessary to correct him.

"That's an interesting costume," Mr. Williams said. "May I ask who you're supposed to be?"

"I'm Vasco da Gama, the European explorer."

"That's different."

"I know. I just did a report on him for school."

"Oh, I see," he said. "Well, good luck and enjoy your candy."

"I sure will. Bye. Thanks."

I walked away thinking that Mr. Williams wasn't scary at all. But how would I tell Kirby that his mom's spirit wasn't coming back?

It was totally dark outside when I closed Mr. William's squeaky gate to head home. Suddenly, a shadowy figure jumped out and yelled at me, causing me to drop my shopping bag of candy.

"Hey! Why did you stop at that spooky guy's house?" I recognized the voice and, thanks to the light of Mr. Williams' lamppost, I saw the third arm.

"What are you doing here, Todd? You scared me half to death."

"I was a few houses behind when I saw you split off from the twins and go in a different direction. I tried to catch up with you to say goodbye. That's when I saw you walk up to the old guy's house. I didn't want to go up to his door because I've heard he's a mean old man. But I decided to wait for you to make sure you got out alive."

I had never realized what a true friend Todd was to me.

"Thanks for watching my back, Todd, but everything is fine. Mr. Williams is not as mean as people think, and my family bought our house from him."

"Still, it was brave of you to walk up to his door," Todd said. "Did he have any candy?"

"Swedish Fish."

"Oh, darn! I love those!"

"Go get some," I said. "Mr. Williams will be happy to have another trick-or-treater, and I'll wait for you here."

"Thanks, Michael. You're the best."

A SACRED SECRET

After returning home from trick-or-treating, I had a Halloween dinner of pepperoni pizza. Then, I went up to my room and dumped my bag of candy on the rug to search for my favorites. I was sitting on the rug sorting the candy when Kirby appeared.

"Wow, that's a lot of candy!" Kirby said. "Which ones do you like best?"

"Pretty much anything with chocolate in it."

"I'd help you eat it," Kirby said, "but I never eat."

"That's okay. I'll have no problem eating it all myself, but it could take a while."

"How did it go with my uncle?" Kirby asked.

"He's not as mean as we thought, and he gave me some candy."

"That surprises me. Were you able to ask him if Mother is coming back?"

"He said she lived a long life and was ready to leave this world."

"Oh. That doesn't sound very hopeful," Kirby said with a sad look on his face.

"Kirby, your uncle also told me how you died."

"Really? Now you probably think that I was stupid for falling down the stairs."

"No, not at all. It was an accident."

"I know, but Mother told me not to fool around, and I didn't listen to her."

"That happens sometimes. When I was five, my mom told me not to wander too far away from her at the beach. But I did and I almost drowned."

"But you survived, and I didn't. Maybe Mother is still mad at me for not listening."

"Kirby, I'm sure your mother loves you. I just wonder how she was able to keep you a secret for so long."

"I think it was difficult for her at first because I didn't want anyone else to know about me. I'm not sure why, but I was afraid that if anyone else saw me, I wouldn't be able to stay with Mother. Keeping our secret was a challenge because, for one thing, Uncle George and Aunt Maggie lived so close to us. Also, Aunt Maggie was an editor of the local newspaper. We were afraid that if she found out about me the whole world would eventually know."

"Do you think anyone ever saw you?" I asked in between bites of a Kit Kat candy bar.

"No, I don't think so because we stuck to our rules. My rule was to never appear in my visible form to anyone but Mother. Many years later, I did try to visit Uncle George in my visible form, but he couldn't see me. So you and my mother are the only people who have ever seen me as a ghost.

"My mother's rule was to never breathe a word about me to anyone. We also kept all the windows in the house covered when I was in my visible form, and we never spoke to each other when we were out of the house and people were around.

"Later on, we discovered that I was still able to use the pogo stick. The problem was that it was noisy when I played with it, and mother was concerned that the neighbors might hear it. That's when she added the rule that I could only jump on the pogo stick in the basement. And that's how we lived until Mother died."

"Wow!" I said. "It's really amazing that your uncle and aunt never saw you. What about your cousin? You never told me about her."

"Do you mean Roseann?"

"Yes, Mr. Williams' daughter."

"I never really knew her. She was born after I died. But Mother told me that Aunt Maggie and Uncle George were always worried about Roseann. They treated her like she was made of sugar and if it rained she would melt. Maybe they were afraid she might die in an accident like I did.

"As Roseann grew up, sometimes I could see her outside our window. Then she went to college, and after that I didn't see her in the neighborhood very much. Mother told me that after Roseann graduated, she worked in downtown Chicago and lived alone. Now, *I'm* alone and I miss Mother."

Kirby looked so seriously sad that I would have done anything to perk him up.

"Don't worry," I said. "I haven't given up on our mission, and neither should you. I'm going to do more research tomorrow and I'll let you know what I find."

"Thanks for not giving up, Michael," Kirby said, sounding more like himself. "I'm going downstairs to play with my pogo stick. I'll come back tomorrow night."

"Are you saying that the pogo stick is still in the basement?"

"Yes, I always hide it under the stairs."

"How do you pick up the pogo stick and jump on it? I didn't think ghosts could do that."

"When I died, I was holding it, and somehow it became a part of me. I can pick it up and jump on it, but I can't take it through walls when I leave the basement. And I can't pick up anything else."

"That's wild. You are just full of interesting stories."

"There are a lot of things people don't know about ghosts," Kirby said. "Maybe you could write them down and pretend that you made them up—I could be your ghostwriter."

"Um, Kirby. Did you know that's a real job? I mean, they're called 'ghostwriters,' but they're not ghosts. A ghostwriter writes for someone else who is named as the author."

"I didn't know," Kirby said. "But how many people have a ghostwriter who's really a ghost?"

"No one, as far as I know."

"Would you like to use my stories?"

"Nah, I don't want to take credit for that."

"Then I guess you'll have to write your own stories. Goodnight, Michael."

"G'night."

PART 5

H ELP

RECAP AT RECESS

"Hey, Vickie. Did you get any good candy last night?" I asked at recess the day after Halloween.

Vickie was standing near the swings, watching some kids playing basketball. It was surprisingly warm outside for the first day of November, and nobody seemed to notice us as we sat on the swings to talk.

"Yeah, I got tons of candy," she said. "How about you?"

"The twins, Todd, and I did really well, and then I went to Mr. Williams' house alone."

"Great! You really did it! How did that go?"

"I haven't told him about Kirby yet, but I did get answers to some of our questions."

"Like what?"

"He said that sometimes strong spirits come back as ghosts because they don't want to let go. I wonder why Kirby's spirit is so strong."

"Maybe it's because he died so young and didn't get a chance to grow up," Vickie said.

"That actually makes a lot of sense. I'm glad we're working on this together."

"Me too," Vickie said. "Did you learn anything else?"

"Yes, Mr. Williams told me how Kirby died."

"Really? What happened?"

"He was jumping on a pogo stick and fell down the basement stairs."

"Oh no! That's horrible!"

"Yeah. And the other bad news is Mr. Williams doesn't think Kirby's mom is coming back as a spirit. He said she was ready to leave this world."

"If she's not coming back, how can we help?" Vickie asked and pulled herself out of the swing.

"I don't know," I said and stood up. "Over the weekend, we should both search the internet to find ways to contact spirits. We can compare notes on Monday."

"Sure, but when can I meet Kirby, like you promised?"

We started walking back to the classroom as the bell rang at the end of recess.

"The next time I see Kirby, I'll tell him that you want to meet him, and we'll work something out."

"Sounds good," Vickie said. "Have a great weekend."

CONFRONTATION ON THE STAIRS

When I came home from school, my mom met me as I walked into the house.

"Remember when I told you I was getting someone to check the furnace?" she asked.

"Yeah."

"So today, the furnace guy came and said there's nothing wrong with it. He couldn't hear any strange sounds, so I guess it's working fine."

"That's good."

"Yeah, but we had to pay for a service call, and the only thing we got out of it was this rusty, old toy the furnace guy found under the stairs in the basement. Do you know what this is?"

When I saw it, time froze for a few seconds before I could talk.

"Um … a pogo stick?"

"Do you want to try it?"

"Not really, I heard those things are dangerous. But it looks cool. Is it okay if I take it up to my room?"

"Sure."

I carried the pogo stick upstairs as my mom walked back into the kitchen. My plan was to stash it under my bed and give it back to Kirby later. But before I got up the stairs, Bryan, wearing gray sweatpants and a torn, black T-shirt, came running downstairs and grabbed the pogo stick out of my hand.

"Give it back!" I yelled at the top of my lungs. "Give it back, you jerk!"

"What is this thing? A pogo stick?" Bryan asked. "Let me try it."

"No! It's mine!" I tried to yank it out of his hands. "You can't have it."

But Bryan held tight, and I felt my face heating up like it was on fire. I was so angry that, without thinking, I hauled off and punched him really hard in his upper left arm.

"Ow! Are you nuts?" Bryan shouted. "What's the matter with you?"

Hearing the commotion, our mom ran back into the living room. "What's going on with both of you?"

"Your younger son just freaked out and punched me in the arm," Bryan said and rushed down the stairs with the pogo stick. "He doesn't want me to play with this piece of junk."

And with that, he threw the pogo stick on the floor with so much force that I thought it would break.

As he walked out of the room toward the kitchen, my mom said, "Don't treat things like that, Bryan. You could scratch the wood floor." *Did she really think Bryan cared about the floor?*

"And Michael, I can't believe you punched your brother. You never do that. Why are you so angry?"

"Bryan grabbed the pogo stick out of my hand when I was walking upstairs and … well, I'm just tired of him picking on me. He's a bully."

"Don't let him get to you. He does things like that to rile you up. If you stop reacting, he'll leave you alone."

"You always say that, and it never changes," I said.

"I wish you two could get along better," she said. "Go to your room and calm down. I'm fixing dinner now, and I'll call you when it's ready."

"All right," I said, as my mom walked back into the kitchen.

Before heading upstairs, I picked up the pogo stick to take with me. It may have been junk to Bryan, but to Kirby it was everything. Fortunately, it wasn't broken.

EMERGENCY ACTION

In my room, I hid the pogo stick under my bed and sat down at my desk. I was still angry at Bryan, so I took a few deep breaths to cool down.

I couldn't believe I hit him. But this was Kirby's pogo stick—the only object he was still able to hold on to in this world. Out of respect for Kirby, I refused to let Bryan take it.

After I cooled down, I did some research for Kirby on my computer.

Vickie's question about what we should do to help Kirby kept running through my head. We needed more information about spirits. I knew my family didn't know much about that stuff, and Mr. Williams and Mrs. Vargas weren't able to help us either. Now, it was time to do our own research.

I had to admit that although Bryan was extremely annoying, he had taught me some valuable things. One of them was how to use the internet to get information for my Vasco da Gama report. Feeling desperate, I started searching for any information I could find about ghosts.

This led me to a blog where most of the posters agreed they didn't know anyone who had died and come back as a ghost. One disagreed and claimed that the spirits of people who died in accidents like to return to the place where they died. This matched Kirby's situation.

To convince ghosts to leave this world, another ghost promoter suggested contacting a medium who could communicate with spirits to let them know it was safe to leave.

I also found a chat group with some weird questions and answers. Someone had asked, "How do I get a ghost out of my house?" The advice included, "politely ask it to leave," "burn sage" (whatever that is), "put salt near the door," and "see a therapist."

None of those answers worked for me because Kirby was my friend. I didn't want to get rid of him; I just wanted Kirby to find his mom. And the therapist comment totally ticked me off, now that I was sure Kirby was real and I wasn't imagining him.

TWO VISITORS

That evening, my dad knocked on my bedroom door while I was doing more research for Kirby.

When he walked in, I was lying on top of my bed, using a study pillow to prop my head and shoulders up as I clicked away on the laptop.

"Mom told me you punched Bryan today," he said. "It's not like you to punch people, and I'm worried. Is everything okay?"

"Yeah."

"Then why did you hit him?"

"Like I already told Mom, I'm tired of being bullied by him."

"Listen, Michael," my dad said and sat down next to me on my bed. "Bryan has always been aggressive and getting into trouble. But you're different. Even before you could talk, I could see that you were intelligent and good natured. Bryan is smart too, but you have qualities that make you a better student."

"But he's better at hockey than me."

"That's true, but did you ever stop to think that maybe you have skills that Bryan wishes he had?"

"That's no reason to pick on me."

"I hope he eventually figures that out," my dad said. "But I think he's making progress because he didn't hit you back."

"That really surprised me," I said.

"Bryan and you are very different from each other, and I hope that someday you'll learn to respect each other more."

"Don't hold your breath," I said.

"I know it's hard for you to believe this right now, but sometimes people can change."

"Yeah, whatever." I didn't think that Bryan would ever change.

"I'll let you get back to what you were doing. Don't stay up too late," my dad said and closed the door as he left my room.

My second visitor that night was Kirby. He showed up in my room after my dad was out of earshot. He looked upset.

"Hey, Kirbster, what's wrong?"

"I can't find the pogo stick. It was under the stairs in the basement, and now I don't know what happened to it."

"I know where it is," I said, as I pulled the pogo stick out from under my bed. "The furnace repair guy found it when he was in the basement, and my mom gave it to me. I was hiding it from Bryan until

I could give it back to you. Don't worry. I didn't tell them about you."

When Kirby saw the pogo stick, he looked relieved. Then we both sat on the bed staring at my computer screen in the dim, orange light of my side-table lamp. He didn't put a dent in the quilt when he sat down.

"How's your research going?" he asked.

All my research was leading to one conclusion. I looked Kirby straight in the eye and said, "Kirby, you're a great friend, and I'd hate to lose you, but I think you need to let go of this world to be with your mother."

That stopped Kirby cold, and I thought he was going to cry. "But I've been here so long and I'm scared to leave."

"I know, but most people who die don't become ghosts. That's why you're so lonely and unhappy here. I want you to be happy."

"Even if I wasn't scared, I don't know how to let go," Kirby said.

"I think Vickie and I need to do more research and talk to your uncle," I said. "He's been around a long time and maybe he can help."

"But he can't see me like you can, and I'm not sure why."

"We'll find a way to make him see you," I said. "And Vickie wants to meet you, too. Is that okay? I was thinking that you, Vickie, and I could all go to your uncle's house together to get more information. I'll talk with her on Monday, and we'll work something out."

"That's fine," Kirby said. "Thanks for wanting to help me. I'm going back to the basement now."

"I'll bring the pogo stick back down to the basement soon," I said, remembering that Kirby couldn't move it through walls or doors. "I can't do it right now because my parents might see me and wonder why I'm taking the pogo stick down to the basement. Early tomorrow morning will work better. Is it okay if I bring it back then?"

"Sure. Goodnight, Michael."

"Goodnight, Kirby. I'll set my clock radio for 5:30 tomorrow morning."

PREDAWN YAWN

"Today will be mostly cloudy, with areas of fog in the morning, and a chance of rain in the afternoon," the weatherman said when the clock radio woke me up at 5:30 the next morning. I turned the radio off right after that, so it wouldn't wake anyone else up on a foggy Saturday morning.

There was nothing even remotely fun about getting up before dawn to take Kirby's pogo stick back to our spooky basement. I would have preferred to stay asleep, but I didn't want to return the pogo stick later, when my family was awake. With a yawn, I grabbed the toy from under my bed and groggily tiptoed down to the basement.

I didn't see Kirby, so I left the pogo stick under the basement stairs and quickly ran up to my room to go back to sleep.

Later that day after dinner, Kirby appeared in my room.

"Thanks for bringing back the pogo stick," he said.

"No problem. But please keep it in a better hiding place in the basement. I don't want anyone to find it again."

"Right. I'll hide it behind the dusty, old bookcases. No one would ever look there."

"That's a good idea," I said. "And don't forget that tomorrow I'm planning to set up a day and time when Vickie, you, and I can walk over to your uncle's house."

"I was thinking about that, but I'm not sure if I'm ready to visit him yet," Kirby said.

"You want to find your mother, don't you?"

"Yes, but do you really think my uncle and Vickie can help us?"

"I'm not sure, but we have to follow every lead."

"I guess so. Just let me know where and when you want to meet," Kirby said. Then he disappeared.

LAST-MINUTE DETAILS

Now that Kirby was on board, I needed to tell Vickie about the meeting plans. The next morning, I saw her on my way to school. She was walking ahead of me, and I ran up to her.

"Kirby is willing to meet you," I said.

"Finally! Where and when?"

"I think it would be best to meet in front of my house with Kirby being invisible. Then the three of us can go over to Mr. Williams' house, where Kirby will become visible. That's when you and Mr. Williams will be able to see him."

"When do you want to do this?" Vickie asked.

"How about tomorrow after school at four o'clock?"

"That's good for me."

"Okay, I'll let Kirby know."

"How does Kirby tell time?" Vickie asked. "He's been around for so long. Do you think he even pays attention to time?"

"When he needs to pay attention, he looks at the clocks in my house."

"Great! Sounds like a good plan for tomorrow," Vickie said, as we walked into the school before the bell rang.

That night, I shared the plan with Kirby. He asked me if I was sure that his uncle would be home when we got to his house. I explained that Mr. Williams was usually home unless he was walking Duke.

Kirby still seemed nervous about seeing his uncle and meeting Vickie, so I told him not to worry and assured him that everything would be fine.

Now, I just needed to convince myself not to worry.

THE DESCENT

After school the next day, I rushed home, ran up to my room to drop off my backpack, and left the house to meet Kirby and Vickie at my front door as planned. On the way out, I told my mom that I was going to visit Mr. Williams. She was fine with that because she had talked to him after Halloween, and he had said nice things about me—the first trick-or-treater to come to his door in many years. She also thought Mr. Williams was lonely and needed company, so I was doing a good deed.

Everything was going smoothly until I walked out the front door and discovered that Vickie wasn't there, and I wasn't sure if invisible Kirby was there either.

"Kirby? Kirby, are you here?" I called out. But there was no response.

A minute later, Vickie came running up the walkway wearing her purple parka and pink stocking cap. She was huffing and puffing as if she had run all the way to my house.

"Sorry I'm late," she said. "I had to help my mother bring groceries into the house before I left. Where's Kirby?"

"He's not here."

"Are you kidding me? He doesn't show up, and you expect me to believe he's real. Is this a joke?"

"I know it looks bad," I said, "but Kirby really does exist. Maybe he's too scared to meet you and see his uncle. I think we're going to have to look for him in my basement."

There was no guarantee that Kirby would be in the basement. But that was the only place I could think of looking. So I reluctantly walked back inside the house with Vickie, and we headed for the basement door near the kitchen.

Fortunately, my mom wasn't around, and Bryan and my dad weren't home to ask what we were doing. I opened the basement door, looked downstairs, and suddenly realized that this was the spot where Kirby had fallen. It gave me the chills to think about how uncertain life could be. At one moment about seventy years ago, Kirby had been at the top of the stairs, and the next moment—disaster.

Shaking that awful thought from my head, I flipped on the basement lights and held on tight to the railing. Vickie followed me as we headed downstairs into the depths of the dark, dank, creepy underbelly of my house.

The basement was a long rectangle, like the footprint of my house. To the left of the staircase was a washer, dryer, and cruddy sink where my mom did laundry. On the right, there was a water heater and furnace. The floor and walls were unfinished and stone gray. The lighting was provided by a few lightbulbs screwed into electric sockets in the ceiling. There also was a tiny bit of sunlight coming through the narrow window wells.

The rest of the basement was full of junk, including old dishes and kitchenware stacked on top of a metal kitchen table. The table looked so old that I thought it probably had belonged to Mrs. Scott. Two tall bookcases full of ancient books stood against the wall behind the table. On the floor, there were several boxes of toys and sports equipment that Bryan and I no longer used, and tons of framed photos and artwork leaned against the walls. At the back wall, there was a wooden door with a couple of locks and a sliding bolt to make sure it was secure. The door led outside to a concrete flight of stairs that went up to our backyard.

I was embarrassed about Vickie seeing my basement because most people had finished basements in the neighborhood. My basement was a dusty, musty place that I had been avoiding since we moved in. Apart from hastily leaving Kirby's pogo stick under the basement stairs a few days before, I had only been down there two or three times when my mom was doing laundry. I imagined that spiders, centipedes, and other creepy bugs with lots of legs lived down there among the cobwebs. It wasn't exactly the best place to bring a guest.

We reached the bottom of the stairs safely, but didn't see Kirby. Trying to find him, I turned to the right just as the furnace kicked on. The noise startled me and made me jump, which made Vickie jump. That's when we heard chuckling coming from under the stairs.

"Hey, Michael, you and your friend are not as brave as I thought," Kirby said in his visible form.

"At least we're not afraid of your uncle like you are," I snapped back. "How come you're hiding under the stairs? I thought you wanted us to help you find your mom. Vickie and I were waiting for you outside."

As soon as I mentioned Vickie, I remembered that this was the first time she had seen Kirby. I knew Vickie could see him because she wasn't moving. It was as if someone had yelled "Freeze!" In her frozen position, she stood next to me staring at Kirby with her eyes and mouth wide open. This lasted for several seconds.

To break the awkward silence, I said, "Kirby, this is my friend Vickie." And I gave her a slight nudge with my elbow to snap her out of her frozen state.

"H-h-hi, K-Kirby," she said. "I-I-I've been looking forward to meeting you."

"Hi, Vickie. Nice meeting you."

"N-n-nice m-meeting you, too."

"Don't worry," Kirby said. "I'm not a scary ghost."

"I know. Michael told me about you," Vickie said, looking more relaxed.

"I'm sorry I didn't show up in front of the house, but I really don't want to talk to my uncle."

"Are you afraid of him?" Vickie asked. "When was the last time you spoke to him?"

"A long time ago, before I died."

"I don't blame you for being scared," Vickie said. "But we can't help you if you don't come with us."

"Why can't the two of you just go and tell him about me?" Kirby asked with a sigh.

"You know that won't work," I said. "How could he believe us without any proof?"

"I guess you're right. But before we go, I want to show both of you something. Come over here."

Kirby led us to the framed photos leaning against the wall near the back of the basement. As we walked toward the photos, I could see some of them were in color, and the older ones were in black and white. I thought they were all photos of my older relatives, but way back in the corner, separated from the rest, was a photo in an antique frame that Kirby was pointing to.

It was dim in the corner, but there was enough light coming through the closest window well for us to see the black-and-white image of Kirby when he was alive. I shivered because he was wearing the same clothes he wore as a ghost. In the photo, he was sitting on a bench next to a standing woman who looked about the same age as my mom. The woman's dark hair was shorter than my mom's and neatly curled, and she wore a formal, dark dress that went below her knees.

"That's Mother," Kirby said. "The photo was taken a few months before I died. It's the only picture of her left in the house. I know it sounds crazy, but sometimes I talk to her photo, because she's not around anymore. I'm glad your family left the photo in the basement, Michael, because it makes me feel good to look at it."

"That's a beautiful picture, Kirby," Vickie said. "I don't think it sounds crazy. I lost my dad last year, and I talk to his photo in my living room all the time. Your mother looks like she was a nice lady."

"She was very nice, and I was with her for many years—first as a boy, and then as a ghost."

Vickie and I stared at the photo for a long time.

"Kirby, how about if we head over to your uncle's house now?" I suggested. "When we get there, I'm going to tell him that Vickie and I have some important questions that would be better to discuss inside his house. Once we're inside, at some point you'll need to become visible so Mr. Williams can see you. I also think we should bring your pogo stick, which

I can carry because I know you can't take it through walls and doors."

"Why do you think we should bring it?" Kirby asked.

"I can't explain it, but I feel there's a special connection between you, your uncle, and the pogo stick."

"You're right!" Kirby said. "He gave it to me before he joined the army."

"WHAT?!" Vickie and I shouted in unison as we looked at each other.

"Yeah, it was a birthday present. I wonder if that's why Uncle George can't see me. Maybe he feels guilty."

"Wow!" Vickie said. "Now I understand why you're afraid to talk to him."

"True. But I don't blame him for the accident," Kirby said.

"And that's exactly what you need to tell your uncle," I said. "Let's go talk to him."

"Okay, I'll meet you at the top of the stairs," Kirby said.

"Promise?" I asked.

"I promise."

But I wasn't sure if I could believe him.

PART 6

H<small>OPE</small>

PART 6: HOPE

BELIEVING IS SEEING

The sky was getting darker as Kirby, Vickie, and I walked to Mr. Williams' house. Kirby was invisible at this point, so I couldn't tell if he was walking or floating. I was holding the pogo stick, worried that Kirby might change his mind at any moment and go back to my house. But he had promised that he would stay with us. I couldn't see him, but I was relieved when he started talking.

"Hey, Vickie," Kirby said. "Do you have any brothers or sisters?"

"Yes, I have a younger sister named Mia."

"You're lucky. I never had a brother or a sister."

"I'm not sure if I'd call that luck," I said.

"I wish you and your brother got along better," Kirby said. "You guys fight all the time."

"That's true—but it's because he picks on me, not the other way around."

"I believe that," Vickie said. "A lot of kids at school think Bryan is a bully."

"Well, I don't want to talk about that right now," I said, thinking about how I had punched Bryan in the arm.

Vickie looked sorry for me, as I opened the gate to Mr. Williams' house.

"Kirby, are you still with us?" I asked.

"Yes, I'm still here in spirit."

"Good. Then let's go." I rang the doorbell, and we heard Duke bark.

A few seconds later, Mr. Williams opened his door and loudly asked, "Who's there?"

"It's me, Michael. You know, I live in your sister's old house."

When Mr. Williams recognized me, he said, "Nice to see you again, Michael. And I see you brought a friend."

I introduced him to Vickie and told him that we had a question about my house.

"Oh, sure. Please come in." As he opened the door wider, I was relieved that he invited us in without me having to ask.

As we walked in, I had to have faith that the invisible Kirby was following us. After Mr. Williams closed the door, I suspected Kirby was in the room because Duke started barking at something behind Vickie and me. It was as if the dog sensed Kirby's presence.

His uncle led us to the living room, which looked like a museum of old furniture and trinkets. It reminded me of the antique store owned by my grandma's friend, and it had the same musty smell.

"So what's the question?" Mr. Williams asked, as he slowly walked to his faded maroon armchair and eased into it. Duke curled up on the floor next to him, and Mr. Williams gestured for Vickie and me to sit on the couch near his armchair.

"It has to do with something that belonged to your nephew, Kirby. Does this look familiar to you?" I asked, holding up the pogo stick so he could see it.

Mr. Williams squinted his eyes as if he couldn't quite recognize it. So I leaned over and held it closer to him in his armchair.

"Good heavens!" he said. "I think that's the pogo stick I gave to Kirby. It's the pogo stick that he … that he …" Mr. Williams couldn't finish his sentence because he was starting to choke up.

"I know," I said. "But there's something else I need to tell you. I hope that you won't think I'm crazy, but the spirit of Kirby is still in my house."

Mr. Williams looked at me and smiled as if I had just told him a joke. "Are you pulling my leg?"

"No, I swear. I'm not kidding. I've met him and so has Vickie."

"I didn't believe Michael at first either," Vickie said. "But it's true."

"Have you told anyone else about this?"

"No, Kirby asked us not to tell anybody," I said. "And to prove that I've met him, he told me some things only you and he would know."

"Like what?" Mr. Williams asked.

"Like how you helped him learn to ride a bike and throw a baseball."

"That's right," Mr. Williams said. "But you could have gotten that information from someone else in the family."

"Where would he get information like that?" Vickie asked. "He's just a kid!"

"Look, Mr. Williams," I said. "You're going to have to believe what you are about to see."

Before Mr. Williams could respond, I shouted, "Kirby! Start jumping!"

With that, Kirby appeared in his visible form, took the pogo stick from me, and started jumping. "Eee-awe, eee-awe, eee-awe," squeaked the pogo stick.

The sound made Mr. Williams and Duke sit up straight and perk up their ears. The squeaking seemed to bother Duke because he started barking and jumping on his hind legs. It looked like he wanted Kirby to stop.

After Kirby stopped jumping, Mr. Williams sat there for a long time looking like a statue. I was sure that he could see Kirby, but I was hoping he wouldn't faint or have a heart attack. And then he put his hands to his face, bent over, and started sobbing. I mean really hard sobbing that made his body shake. Kirby walked over to comfort him.

"Oh, Kirby. Is it really you?" Mr. Williams asked, wiping the tears from his eyes. "I thought I saw you once a long time ago, but I didn't want to believe that you were a ghost. I feared that if I saw you, I'd go mad, because it was my fault that you died. I never should have given you that pogo stick. I'm so sorry. I've really missed you."

"I don't blame you for the accident," Kirby said. "But I could never understand why you couldn't see me."

Things were getting emotional, and I was feeling uncomfortable and a little embarrassed to be listening to such a personal conversation. Vickie didn't seem as uncomfortable. She was listening carefully and taking it all in with a sad look on her face.

"Mr. Williams," I said, "Kirby really needs your help. That's why we're here."

"How can I help?" Mr. Williams asked, trying to hold back his tears.

"You see, Kirby wants to be with his mother's spirit, and he doesn't know how to find her," I said. "We're trying to help him, but we don't know what to do. We were hoping that you'd have an idea."

From his armchair, Mr. Williams thought about this for a moment and said, "I don't know what to do either."

"But I thought you, Mother, and Grandmamma knew how to talk to spirits," Kirby said.

"Well, when my father—your grandfather—died, my mother contacted a medium. That's someone who can connect with spirits. She wanted the medium to conduct a séance to communicate with my father. But it didn't work."

"Grandmamma said that if a dead person doesn't come back as a spirit within a year of their death …"

"Yes, I know," Mr. Williams interrupted. "…they won't come back at all. That's something the medium told her, but I don't know if it's true."

"But if it *is* true, that means I have to find Mother's spirit soon, and it's already November."

"Kirby, I really want to help you," Mr. Williams said. "But I need more time to think about this. Would you be able to stay with me for a few days?"

"That would be wonderful!" Kirby said. "I have so many questions about the past that I want to ask you."

I was so moved to see Kirby and Mr. Williams reunited that I almost started to tear up.

"I guess we should be going," Vickie said.

As Vickie and I walked out the front door, I told Kirby and Mr. Williams that I'd check back with them in a few days.

There was a chill in the air as we walked back to my house.

"That was unbelievable!" Vickie said.

"I know. Kirby handled it so well. I'm glad that they are going to spend a few days getting to know each other again."

"That's great," Vickie said. "And it probably wouldn't have happened without your idea to bring the pogo stick with us."

"I'm glad it worked, but now I just hope that Mr. Williams can help Kirby."

"You know, I was thinking about that," Vickie said. "Do you know where Kirby first appeared as a ghost?"

"Yep. It was at the graveyard where he was buried."

"Is his mother buried there, too?"

"Probably."

"Maybe that's where we should look for more clues," Vickie said, as we reached my house.

"Not a bad idea," I said, even though it sounded scary. "On Saturday, I'll ask Kirby and Mr. Williams where the tombstones are located."

"Let me know what you find out," Vickie said and headed for home.

PART 7

HISTORY

PART 7: HISTORY

A GRAVE PLAN!

Three days after Vickie and I had left Kirby with Mr. Williams, I returned like I promised. I brought the framed, black-and-white photo of Mrs. Scott and Kirby from my basement, because I thought Kirby would be missing it and Mr. Williams would like to scc it.

When I arrived, Mr. Williams opened the door, thanked me for the photo, and led me into the living room, where Kirby and Duke were waiting.

"Hey, Cousin!" Kirby yelled when he saw me.

"Hey, Kirby," I said. "Why'd you call me 'cousin'?"

"We've got a surprise for you," Kirby replied. "Uncle George has been doing some research since I got here."

"That's right," Mr. Williams said, as he eased into his armchair and directed Kirby and me to sit on the couch. "I was looking at some family documents from the 1930s, and I found two family tree diagrams that Kirby's mom, Caroline, had created. She must have done these around the time she married Kirby's dad, Frank Scott, because one tree was for the Williams Family and the other was for the Scott

Family. It turns out that Kirby and your grandfather, Martin Coin, are second cousins."

"How do you know?" I asked.

"Because a long time ago, a Coin married a Scott. That makes you and Kirby distant cousins."

"No wonder we get along so well," I said, as Kirby and I exchanged grins. "That's amazing!"

"I know," Kirby said. "But now I have to tell you the bad news. We have a serious problem. Uncle George told me that I was wrong about the date my mother died. I thought it was in December of last year, but it was really on the tenth of November. Like I said, I'm not that good with dates. That means the one-year deadline for her to come back as a ghost is this Sunday."

"Oh no!" I said. "This is an emergency."

"What can we do?" Kirby asked desperately.

"You know," I said, "Vickie thought we might find more clues if we went to the cemetery where Mrs. Scott is buried."

"She's buried in the church cemetery about a half-mile down the road," Mr. Williams said. "Kirby's grave and tombstone are also there."

"Hmm, I think we really need to go to the cemetery," I said. "I'm busy tomorrow, but maybe we could all walk there on Sunday afternoon."

"Do you think we'll find some clues about Mother when we get there?" Kirby asked.

"Ever since we started this mission," I said, "I've learned that we have to try everything we can. This is our best shot. Are you willing to try?"

"Yes," Kirby said, as he got off the couch and floated over to his uncle. "How about you, Uncle George?"

"Fine. What kind of clues are you looking for?" Mr. Williams asked.

"Any hints that ghosts have been there," I said.

"I don't know if you'll find anything," Mr. Williams said standing up slowly. "But stop by my house on Sunday at two o'clock with Vickie, if she's available, and we'll all walk over to the church together."

A thought occurred to me as I stood up and prepared to leave. "It's important that we bring the pogo stick," I said. "I'm not sure why, but it may help us at the cemetery."

"No problem. We'll bring it with us," Kirby said, as he, Mr. Williams, and Duke followed me to the front door.

"You know, you're amazingly smart for your age," Mr. Williams told me.

"Me? No, it's just that I've never had friends like you and Kirby, and I want to help."

"Caroline would be pleased to know that such a nice boy moved into her house," Mr. Williams replied.

"Thanks," I said, a little embarrassed by the praise. "Then it's all set. I'll meet you here on Sunday at two o'clock, and I'll see if Vickie can join us."

"Great," Kirby said.

"Oh! I almost forgot," Mr. Williams said. "Here's something I thought you might like to read."

On the table near his front door, Mr. Williams picked up what looked like an ancient notebook. "As I was going through those old family documents," he said, "I found this journal that my wife, Maggie, wrote. She was a writer for our local newspaper, the *Long Field Leader*, and took notes about everything. Kirby said that you like history, so I thought you'd be interested in her notes about our family."

"Cool!" I said. "Before Halloween, I wrote a family history for my English class. That's how I got interested in family stories, and it would be great to read yours."

"You can take the notebook home to read, but please bring it back on Sunday," Mr. Williams said.

"Thanks, Mr. Williams."

"I hope everything works out on Sunday," Kirby said.

"We'll try our best," I said. But I was worried that we were running out of time.

On my way home, I wondered what would happen if Kirby couldn't find his mother. Would he stay with his uncle? And what would he do after Mr. Williams died—come back to my house?

It was great having Kirby around, because he was like a brother who was nice to me. But I was getting older every day, and Kirby was stuck at eleven years old. Eventually, I was planning to go to college. What would Kirby do then?

I knew Kirby was unhappy without his mother. At the same time, he was scared to leave this world and look for her on the other side. This left Kirby stuck in the middle.

My teacher would call it "a dilemma." To get him unstuck, I wanted to help him in any way I could. Kirby was desperate.

THE WILLIAMS CLAN

That night, I read Maggie Williams' notebook in bed before I fell asleep. I was tired, but once I started reading it, I couldn't put it down. It explained so much of the early history of Kirby and Mr. Williams.

Her notes started in 1928, when she became friends with Kirby's mom, and met Caroline's two brothers—Mickey and George Williams. This was a long time before Maggie married George.

Maggie described Caroline as being very pretty and friendly. Mickey, who was two years younger than Caroline and two years older than George, was a troublemaker. George was "a nice guy" and the opposite of Mickey.

Mickey's best friend, Frank Scott, was also in the picture. He was a troublemaker like Mickey. For some reason, George hung around with Mickey and Frank, even though he was so different. Caroline called them "The Three Musketeers."

In 1932, Caroline married Frank, who worked as an auto mechanic. Caroline, who was two years older than Frank, had graduated from nursing school and worked at the local hospital. According to Maggie's notes, George was secretly worried that the marriage wouldn't work out.

Kirby was born in 1934, and Frank moved to Southern California a year later. It sounded like he figured he could be a mechanic anywhere, so he left to start a new life in a sunnier climate, leaving Caroline and Kirby behind.

This was really hard on Caroline, but it gave George the opportunity to be a substitute father for Kirby. George was there when Kirby learned to walk, and later taught him many things like how to throw a baseball. He also liked buying special presents for Kirby.

In 1938, George bought the house with the white picket fence on Oakland Avenue. He was an accountant, and according to Maggie, "The house was perfect for getting married and starting a family." But George remained a bachelor and worked long hours for his clients.

George was still a bachelor when Japan attacked Pearl Harbor, Hawaii, on December 7, 1941, causing the United States to enter World War II. Two weeks later, Caroline and George's father died, which left

Caroline, Kirby, and Kirby's grandmother all living together in a house a few doors away from George. To support the family, Caroline still worked as a nurse, while Kirby's grandmother looked after him.

In early 1943, George joined the army. The night before he left for boot camp, George gave Kirby a special birthday present—a pogo stick that Kirby was excited to get.

During the war, George fought in an infantry unit in Europe. As the United States and their allies started closing in on Hitler, everyone back home hoped that their loved ones overseas would return soon.

According to Maggie, our town of Long Field lost too many men in the war. But the most heartbreaking event for George and his family happened in April 1945. As a family friend, Maggie sent this letter to George in Europe:

April 17, 1945
Dear George,

I'm so sorry to have to tell you this, but your family asked me to let you know that Kirby had a serious accident and died. He fell down the basement stairs and broke his neck. Your mother and sister are in shock, and I'm doing everything I can to help. Under these circumstances, is there any way you can come home early? We all miss you and hope to see you soon.

Sincerely,

Maggie

George later told Maggie that he went into shock after reading her letter. He said it was like a shell exploded inside his head. He couldn't eat; he couldn't sleep; and he could hardly function. According to Maggie, "At first, he considered asking for compassionate leave from the army to help his family, but he eventually decided to stick with his comrades until the war ended."

By Thanksgiving 1945, George was discharged from the U.S. Army, and he returned home. As he settled back into civilian life, Maggie encouraged him to have a heart-to-heart talk with his sister about Kirby's death. Later, Maggie learned that when they finally spoke, Caroline told her brother the whole story about how Kirby fell down the basement stairs when he was jumping on the pogo stick that George had given him. Maggie noted that George was never able to forgive himself for buying Kirby that cursed pogo stick.

In the summer of 1946, George and Maggie were married. They celebrated the birth of their daughter, Roseann, a year later. A few months after Roseann's birth, Caroline and George's mother died, leaving Caroline alone in her house. Maggie often wondered why Caroline never remarried and seemed perfectly happy living alone.

After reading Maggie's notes, I fell asleep dreaming about World War II, based on the photos and movies I had seen.

PART 8

Hockey

PART 8: HOCKEY

A SECRET MISSION

"Hello, Mrs. Vargas," I said, calling from my home phone on Saturday afternoon. "This is Michael Benton. Is Vickie home?"

"Hi, Michael. Yes, she's here. We just got back from her dance class."

"Could I speak with her for a minute?"

"Of course, I'll get her."

Standing in my kitchen, I nervously waited for Vickie to come to the phone. I was worried that someone in my family might walk into the room and listen to my conversation. When Vickie came to the phone, she sounded surprised. But that made sense because it was the first time I had ever called her.

"Hi!" she said. "I didn't know you had my phone number."

"I found it in the school directory that my mom got from the PTA. Listen. I need to ask you a question, but not over the phone. Can I come to your house for a few minutes? I'll ride over on my bike. When I get there, it would be better if we talked outside."

"Okay, I'll watch for you out the window."

"Great. I should be there in about five minutes."

It was about three o'clock in the afternoon when I rode to Vickie's house. As I peddled, I thought about her idea to look for clues at the cemetery to help reunite Kirby with his mom. Vickie didn't know this, but I had a huge fear of cemeteries ever since I almost drowned. Whenever I was *near* a cemetery, it reminded me that I almost ended up *in* one.

The woman in the white gown, who I saw underwater, had told me, "Don't be afraid, just believe in yourself." I wanted to follow her advice to overcome my fear. And I knew I'd feel more confident if Vickie was able to join me at the cemetery on Sunday. After all, the whole idea started with Vickie's suggestion that we visit the place where Mrs. Scott was buried.

The problem was I hadn't told Vickie about the emergency graveyard meeting yet. During a school day, it was easy to talk to her, especially at lunch or at recess. But today was Saturday, so after hockey practice, lunch with my family, and doing chores, I had decided to give her a call.

I had set up the in-person meeting to talk to her about Kirby because I was afraid that someone in her family or my family might overhear us if we talked over the phone.

It was cold outside when I rode my bike to Vickie's house. Fortunately, there was no ice or snow on the streets, and I was wearing my warm winter jacket, so it wasn't too bad. Vickie was waiting outside her house when I arrived.

"What's up?" she asked. "I'm guessing it's about Kirby."

"Good guess. I met with Kirby and Mr. Williams yesterday, and we've got an emergency. Kirby found out that tomorrow is the one-year anniversary of his mother's death. If we don't do something by then, it may be too late for his mother to come back as a ghost. So I told them about your idea to go to the cemetery where Mrs. Scott is buried, and they agreed to come along. I was wondering if you could also join us tomorrow."

"Why do you need me there?"

"Because you've helped me so much with this, and I'd like you to be there. We'd need to meet at Mr. Williams' house at two o'clock."

"I should be home from church by then, so I think I can join you. But, because it would be weird to tell my mother that I'm going to a cemetery, I'll tell her I'm going to your house to do homework."

"That's a good idea," I said.

"Okay, I better go in now. I'm freezing," Vickie said. "I'll see you tomorrow, and I hope everything works out for Kirby."

"Me too. Bye."

TIME CONFLICT

I was pleased with the way things were shaping up for our trip to the cemetery until I hit a snag on Sunday morning. That's when my mom reminded me about the annual hockey potluck party to be held at Billy and Brad's house that afternoon. The party was planned for around the same time as the cemetery visit. It was a party for all the families in our hockey league to boost team spirit for the upcoming hockey season.

I didn't know what to do. Today was Kirby's deadline, so I couldn't postpone the cemetery visit.

"Um, do I have to go?" I asked my mom in desperation.

"Of course! How would it look if Dad, Bryan, and I went without you, especially because you're such good friends with Billy and Brad?"

She was right, I had to be there.

"So what should we bring to the potluck lunch?" my mom asked.

"Kids really like salsa and chips," I suggested. "What do you think?"

"That's a good idea," my mom said. "I'm going to the store now. I'll get salsa and chips, and if I find something else that looks good, I'll get that, too. Bye."

As soon as she left, I looked at the clock. It was ten o'clock and the party was going to start at noon. I considered my options.

Earlier that morning, I had seen Mr. Williams leave for church with his daughter, Roseann. And I knew that Vickie and her family would also be at church. That meant I wouldn't be able to get the word out to either of them in time before I left for the hockey party.

I was starting to panic, when I remembered that Todd—the boy with the Martian suit—lived across the street from the twins' house where the party was being held. That gave me an idea.

FAVOR FROM A FRIEND

I knew Todd wouldn't be at the party because he didn't play hockey. He preferred playing video games, which he was very good at. He was also good at math. Vickie and I would sometimes work with him in class to solve hard math problems as a team.

Right after my mom left for the store, I called Todd on the phone.

"Todd, are you going to be home this afternoon?"

"I could be. Why?"

"I was wondering if we could work on our math homework together. I could use some help."

"Sure. What time?"

"I can ride my bike to your house at around four o'clock."

"That's good. See you then."

Now that I had a plan in place, I just hoped the timing would work out.

THE PARTY

"I'm going to ride my bike over to the twins' house for the party," I told my family as they were getting ready to drive over to Billy and Brad's house.

"Why can't you come with us?" my dad asked.

"Because after the party, I'm going over to Todd's house to do math homework."

"What a couple of nerds!" Bryan said. "Always doing homework."

"It wouldn't kill you if you did a little more homework yourself," my mom told Bryan.

"See you at the party, Michael," my dad said.

As my family drove away, I took off on my bike. My math book and the notebook Mr. Williams gave me were in my backpack.

These hockey potlucks were always the same. On a big table in the dining room, the parents had set up the lunch that included chips, dips, pizza, pasta, garlic bread, and chocolate chip cookies. Meanwhile, all the kids were in the basement, playing air hockey, ping-pong, or video games.

Right before the buffet lunch started, everyone squeezed into the dining room, where Coach Weekly gave his usual words of encouragement for the new season. His speech ended with, "I want to thank all of our families for supporting our junior hockey league. These boys have been working hard at practices, so let's do some serious skating and winning this year!"

After the applause for the speech, we all swarmed the table, grabbed our food, and devoured everything. I watched the clock carefully as I ate.

At 1:30 p.m., I told my parents that I was heading over to Todd's. At that point, they didn't mind me leaving early because I had been there long enough. When I walked toward the front door with my backpack, my brother and two of his friends saw me leaving.

"Hey, Bro! Where are you going?" Bryan asked, even though he thought he knew.

I just smiled and kept walking.

"Do you have a math date with your little nerd friend?" Bryan continued. His buddies laughed.

At that moment, I remembered that the underwater lady had told me to believe in myself. Suddenly, I knew exactly what to do. I didn't take the bait. Instead, I walked out without saying a word.

PART 9

HOME

PART 9: HOME

TRUTH BE TOLD

I really didn't go to Todd's house to do homework, or at least not right away. Instead, I zoomed over to Mr. Williams' house on my bike to meet him and Kirby as planned. Vickie was waiting for me near the white picket fence. She had her purple backpack over her shoulders, so I knew she had her homework with her.

"Hi, Vickie," I said, hiding my bike behind Mr. Williams' bushes. "Thanks for coming."

"No problem. My mom was fine with me leaving the house after I told her that I was going to do homework with you."

"Well, if you're interested," I said, as we walked up to the front door, "I'm planning to do math homework with Todd later this afternoon. Do you want to join us?"

"Sure. That way it wouldn't be a lie."

"But first, we have to finish our secret mission," I said and rang the doorbell.

"I just hope we're successful," Vickie said. "We're running out of time."

FIRST SNOW

A few seconds later, Mr. Williams opened the door and welcomed us in. Kirby and Duke were standing nearby.

"Thanks for letting me read this," I said, as I handed Maggie's notebook back to Mr. Williams. "It was interesting to learn more about you and Kirby."

"You're welcome," Mr. Williams said. "Vickie, would you like to read it?"

"Sure!"

Mr. Williams smiled and handed her the notebook. "Please return it when you're done."

"I will. Thanks," Vickie said, sliding the notebook into her backpack.

"We should get going," I said.

"I just need a minute to put my coat on and get Duke's leash," Mr. Williams said.

"I'll stay invisible on the way to the cemetery," Kirby said.

"Do you want me to carry your pogo stick?" I asked.

"That would be great." I could tell Kirby was trying to make the best of things, but he looked worried. He gave me his pogo stick and then went invisible.

With pogo stick in hand, I joined Mr. Williams, Duke, invisible Kirby, and Vickie as we walked out the door to start our half-mile journey. I was nervous about going to the cemetery, but it helped to be with friends.

It was now the tenth of November, and right before we reached the cemetery, a light snow began to fall. This was the first snow of the season. As we watched the flakes fall, Kirby reappeared.

"You know, Kirby," Mr. Williams said, "your mother always loved the snow."

"I remember that," Kirby said, as we reached the entrance to the cemetery. "When I was alive, Mother took me sledding whenever there was enough snow. She enjoyed it as much as I did."

A tall metal fence surrounded the cemetery. When we walked inside the gate, there was a deep silence that I wasn't used to hearing—or rather, not hearing. There were crooked, cracked, and neglected gravestones everywhere. And large, gnarly trees with no leaves stood guard over this silent place.

Mr. Williams directed us to his sister's gravestone, which was right next to Kirby's gravestone.

Mrs. Scott's gravestone read:

Caroline Williams Scott

Loving daughter, sister, mother, aunt, and friend

Rest in Peace

Using Kirby's given name, his gravestone read:

Curtis Williams Scott

A moment in our arms, forever in our hearts

Rest in Peace

I had just read those words, when Mr. Williams said, "I can't believe it's already a year since my sister's death. I know Kirby misses her, but I miss her, too. I have so many great memories of us growing up together, but that seems like a thousand years ago."

"Do you think she knows we're here?" Kirby asked.

"I'd like to think so," Mr. Williams said. "I'm going to walk over and pay my respects to other relatives who are buried here, including my mother and father. Kirby, would you like to join me?"

"Sure," Kirby said. "Michael, I'll take the pogo stick now."

After Kirby took the pogo stick, he, Mr. Williams, and Duke walked to the other graves.

"We better seriously start looking for clues," Vickie told me. "I'm going to check out those cracked tombstones near the gate."

"I'll start looking, too," I said, as she walked away. "Let me know if you find anything."

The deadline to find Kirby's mom was creeping up on us. I lost my fear of the cemetery because I was so desperate to help Kirby. The problem was, I didn't know what to look for. Should I search for spirits popping out of the ground? Should I look for green slime like in the *Ghostbusters* movies? I wasn't sure.

As I searched for anything I could find around Kirby and Mrs. Scott's tombstones, Kirby came back to his mother's grave. He was still holding the pogo stick. I started to wonder if that toy had special powers of its own. Did the power of the pogo stick help Mr. Williams finally see Kirby as a ghost? Did the pogo stick have control over me when I punched Bryan for snatching it? If it had that much power, maybe it would work here.

"Kirby," I said, "if you jump on the pogo stick, maybe something will happen."

"Like what?" he asked.

"Like attract your mom's spirit to come back or take you to the other side."

"I'll try it," Kirby said. "We're running out of time!"

"I know," I said. "But, just in case you end up on the other side, we should say goodbye."

"You're a true friend, Cousin Michael," Kirby said. "I appreciate everything you've done for me. I may never see you again, but I hope you have a good life and live to an old age."

"Thanks, Kirby. I've learned so much from you. I'm going to miss you if you leave, but I know how happy you'll be to find your mother."

"Thanks, Michael. I'll never forget you."

"I'll never forget you either," I said.

With that, Kirby started jumping near his mother's grave. "Eee-awe, eee-awe, eee-awe," squeaked the pogo stick.

As he jumped, he cried out, "Mother, please! Mother, please!"

Mr. Williams and Vickie joined us to see what was going on.

"Why is Kirby jumping like that?" Vickie asked.

"He's trying to make contact with his mother's spirit," I said, "but nothing's happening."

Kirby started to cry as he jumped. To ease his pain and disappointment, Mr. Williams, Vickie, and I walked closer to him.

As soon as we reached him, we saw a funnel cloud of snow heading toward us. We all huddled together as the wind picked up, and the snow cloud swirled around us like a soft, white blanket.

Inside this whirlwind, my eyes were closed, but I thought I heard a woman sigh softly. That's when Mr. Williams yelled, "Caroline and Kirby! I hope to see you on the other side some day!"

I wanted to see what was happening, so I opened my eyes. The wind was howling, and I was almost blinded by the snow. As I looked closer, I saw a familiar face, but it wasn't Kirby or his mother. It was the lady in white who spoke to me underwater when I almost drowned. Only this time, her gown was made of the snow that was swirling around us. Without speaking, she just looked at me and smiled. Then her face faded into the windblown snow.

A few seconds later, the wind died down, and KIRBY WAS GONE!

BETTER LEFT UNSAID

After the storm, I felt shaken up and stunned by the experience. I was sure that Mr. Williams, Vickie, and even Duke were feeling the same way.

All that remained on the spot where we last saw Kirby was a dusting of snow and his pogo stick. I guess he didn't need to take it with him.

The first person to move was Mr. Williams, who slowly picked up the pogo stick. That was our signal to start walking back to his house. We walked silently at first, and then started to talk.

"Did either of you see what happened right before Kirby disappeared?" I asked.

"I didn't see anything," Vickie said. "My eyes were closed because it was so windy and the snow was blowing in my face."

"I thought I saw Caroline and Kirby holding hands before they walked away and vanished," Mr. Williams said. "I wonder if it was the snow or the pogo stick that brought them back together. I guess we'll never know."

"Michael, did you see Caroline and Kirby in the storm?" Vickie asked.

"No, I didn't see them."

"Maybe I imagined it or I was the only one who could see them," Mr. Williams said. "I believe some things happen in this world that can't be explained."

"Out of respect for Kirby," Vickie said, "I don't want to tell anyone about this, but I'm really glad that I met him."

"The last few days I spent with Kirby brought back old memories and feelings that I had ignored for a long time," Mr. Williams said.

"What kind of feelings?" Vickie asked.

"Feelings of happiness, excitement, love, sadness … it made me feel more alive."

"Kirby helped me with my feelings about losing my dad," Vickie said. "I understood why he missed his mother so much, and I learned that it's okay to feel that way."

"How about you, Michael?" Mr. Williams asked. "What did you learn?"

"I learned the importance of trusting my friends and believing in myself," I said. "And I agree with you that some things can't be explained."

I decided not to tell them about the lady in white, who visited me twice—first in waves and then in snow. That was a secret I wasn't ready to share.

It was almost four o'clock when we reached Mr. Williams' house, and the sun was lower in the sky. I grabbed my bike from behind his bushes and said, "Goodbye, Mr. Williams. I'll come back to visit you and Duke soon."

Waving goodbye from his stoop, Mr. Williams said, "Bye, Michael! Bye, Vickie! Thanks for everything!"

"Bye," Vickie said. "I'll never forget this day."

And with backpacks on our shoulders, and me walking my bike, Vickie and I went to Todd's house to do math homework.

A RATTLE AND A WINK

Almost three weeks later, I celebrated Thanksgiving Day at home with my brother, parents, and grandparents, as usual. But this year, my mom also invited Mr. Williams and his daughter, Roseann, who was the same age as my grandparents.

As we welcomed them into our house, I could see that Mr. Williams was holding the pogo stick.

"I think you left this at my house," he said, giving it back to me.

"Oh, yay!" Bryan said in his usual sarcastic voice. "Michael's precious pogo stick is back, and—believe me—I know what happens when you get between Michael and that pogo stick."

"It's important to me," I said.

"I know," Bryan said. "Don't worry, I'm not going to mess with it."

My parents looked pleased when they heard that. It was a glimmer of hope.

As we sat down at the Thanksgiving table, I had a warm feeling inside. It was good to be at home with these people—even Bryan. Then I thought about how important being with family was to Kirby. I hoped that he was now with his mother and he was happy. Deep in these thoughts, I suddenly heard the wind rattle the dining room window, making a noise that almost sounded like Kirby's pogo stick.

As I looked up toward the window, Mr. Williams winked at me.

ACKNOWLEDGMENTS

I am grateful for the encouragement, friendship, love, understanding, and so much more that I received from my family and friends: Denise Cella, Lou Cella, Ondine Cella, Eleanor Gliane, Nicole Hammonds, Sheri Hammonds, Hugh Iglarsh, Judith Iglarsh, Bill Kirkpatrick, Ricky Kirkpatrick, Cheryl Kobetsky, Don Kobetsky, Bill Lawless, Siri Micari-Lawless, Joy Mix, Ivania Olivares, Jason Rose, Lisa Rose, Bob Spector, Daira Tramontin, and Vera VonHoldenberg. And I want to specially thank my Critinomicon friends: Phil Bloch, Judy Bond, Rich Chwedyk, Mike Pickard, Lisa Roberts, and Leslie Schwartz.